A Deadly Combination

Where Darkness Reigns

Bianca's Story

Book 1

By: Mary Reason Theriot

Dedication

A very special thank you to Louis Dupuy for not only helping me come up with the idea for this particular book, but taking the time to let me bounce ideas off of him, no matter how far fetched they may have seemed at the time.

Without the love and support of my family and friends, I would not have pursued this new path in life. I would especially like to thank those that have proofread copy after copy, to give me their honest opinion of the books.

Theresa, thank you so much for your continued encouragement. Without you, some of the characters would not have "come to life."

To my wonderful husband Malwen, your continued love and support mean the world to me. I don't know what I would do without you in my life. One of these nights I'm sure you will be able to sleep with both eyes closed. Eventually, I should run out of ideas… or maybe not. These books wouldn't be what they are without you pushing me forward.

To Don Reason and Malcolm "Phil" Theriot for sharing your knowledge and experience of law enforcement protocol.

To my fans, I would like to offer a special thank you for your continued support.

This book is a work of fiction. Names, characters, places and incidents are the product of the author's imagination and are used fictitiously. Any resemblance to actual persons, living or dead, events or places are entirely coincidental.

Also Available by Mary Reason Theriot:

The Hideaway
The Traveler
Dr. Frankenstein
Above Suspicion
Horror in the Night
Deadly Seduction
Echoes on the Bayou
Seven Deadly Sins
A Kiss So Deadly
CarnEvil of Souls
Seduced by Voodoo
Haunted Visions
Unrequited Love

www.maryreasontheriot.com

Now Available on AudioBook:

A Deadly Combination

Dear Reader,

There are some characters that I loved so much that they had to be brought back. *Where Darkness Reigns* contains some of my favorite characters who had to meet and join forces with other characters.

Bianca Honore's story begins in A Deadly Combination, but when she partners with Joshua Savoie in Seduced by Voodoo you learn that her heart and soul are just as black as the voodoo she practices.

Joshua Savoie's story begins in CarnEvil of Souls, but, as in life, true evil never dies but remains hidden until the opportune moment. Joshua comes back in Seduced by Voodoo to see his diabolical plan come to fruition.

Rayne Simoneaud is betrayed by her lover, Dominic St Germaine, in A Deadly Combination, but seeks out her revenge in Seduced by Voodoo.

Josie Bellows is a young vamp from CarnEvil of Souls who searches for the vampire who turned her so that she can find Redemption.

Detective Grace Hutcherson has fought vampires in CarnEvil of Souls, survived the battle of good versus evil in Seduced by Voodoo and now finds herself plagued by Haunted Visions.

***

CarnEvil of Souls – Joshua's Story
A Deadly Combination – Bianca's Story
Seduced by Voodoo – Lovers Unite
Redemption – Josie's Story
Haunted Visions – Detective Grace Hutcherson's Story

Introduction

A Brief History of the St. Germaine Family

Jacque St. Germaine was a simple boy that desperately needed work. He ran errands for Mr. Ramon Gambini while the Louisiana sun beat down on his neck and the hot asphalt melted the soles of his shoes. Still, he did his errands without a word of complaint, which impressed Mr. Gambini. There was no task the young boy wouldn't get done.

Over the years, as Jacque St. Germaine became more familiar with the Gambini Family business, he moved up to being a bagman. He was entrusted to pick up loan and protection payments. As a soldier, Jacque St. Germaine carried a set of brass knuckles that he used on those who could not pay. To this day, his great, great grandson and current Boss, Dominic St. Germaine, carries them in his pocket.

In the Mafia, when a member of The Family committed their first clip (murder) it was known as "making your bones". Jacque made his bones at the tender age of fifteen. By committing this clip, he proved his loyalty to Mr. Gambini and The Family.

Years later, Phillip Morella, the police commissioner for the City of New Orleans, had refused to accept any bribes, which infuriated Mr. Gambini. When Jacque clipped Phillip Morella, he quickly made rank as Mr. Gambini's underboss. This significant promotion meant he was now the Boss' most trusted right-hand man and second-in-command. If Mr. Gambini were killed or imprisoned, Jacque would assume the duties as The Boss.

In 1902, Jacque St. Germaine took over for the Gambini Family. That year he purchased an old, run down hotel in the French Quarter and turned it into one of the most popular hotels in New Orleans. As soon as he did that, his competitors saw the brilliance and followed suit. However, their Family's hotel became one of the finest hotels in the French Quarter in record time. The penthouse suite became home for Jacque St. Germaine, where he lived for many years. Jacque St. Germaine made sure that his penthouse suite was the finest. No expense had been spared when he furnished the place.

Typically the structure of the Mafia had rules implemented to prevent nepotism in the ranks. Membership and rank in the Mafia were not a birthright, and new Bosses should not be related to their predecessor. Some Mafia Families forbid relatives from holding positions in that Family at the same time. However, when Jacque St. Germaine took over as Boss, he wanted to bring his sons into the trade, with the eldest taking his position as Boss when the time came. From there it became a Family tradition that the eldest son took over as Boss.

The Family's longest running and most profitable venture from the beginning was protecting "clients" from theft. From there they ventured into racketeering and other areas such as bootlegging. The Prohibition era in the 1920s provided The Family the best opportunity to flourish.

As commerce and trade picked up in New Orleans, they offered clients the option to threaten their competition with 'force'. If two businessmen happened to be competing for a bid on a contract, the client sometimes asked the Family to "convince" the rival to drop out of the bidding process. The Family could be convinced to pressure local restaurants and bars into carrying their client's products.

Another profitable business venture was loan sharking. Over thirty percent of small businesses here were indebted to his Family and with the current state of the economy, that number had increased drastically. Companies and individuals came to them since the banks had tighter lending practices.

Each new Boss of the Family would start a new business venture. His grandfather helped the business grow even bigger by cashing in on the construction industry and obtaining payoffs for not only certain government contracts but private contracts as well. His grandfather had gotten this idea when a politician requested help to obtain votes during his election. His grandfather's endorsement had been enough to help that politician win the election. The politician repaid his debt by helping with any contract and permit that his grandfather needed. Vote buying turned into another lucrative venture as The Family asked clients, relatives and associates to vote for a certain candidate. Those politicians in turn repaid the favor in cash or with a particular favor such as helping to sabotage a police investigation or awarding a needed contract or permit. Over the years, they received kickbacks from quite a few influential politicians and badges (law enforcement officials).

Recently they had begun to infiltrate several banks in smaller towns. This had been a smart move on their part. It provided them the perfect cover to launder money without having to answer a lot of questions.

Presidents and other members on the bank boards were so greedy that they could easily be coerced into "helping" his Family get what they needed. Once they moved into a small town, it was usually easy to convince the town mayor and others to turn the other way when they, or their business associates, came into town. Occasionally, they did have a mayor or chief of police who refused to cooperate. However, when the next election came around, they made sure to buy enough votes to get that mayor or chief of police out of office.

Several land owners greedily accepted money for the use of their land. They didn't care how they used the land, and never asked. If they became curious, they were quickly quieted.

One of their latest ventures was acquiring casinos and turning New Orleans into an international gambling mecca. This gave them an increased influx of money. His Family also controlled most of the waterfront commerce in the port of New Orleans, which allowed them more control of the port. It quickly became known that whenever a shipment came into New Orleans, a fee must be paid to The Family to dock on the area of the port they owned.

The club where the business started still stood and had changed very little. The interior of the club remained dark and smoke filled. No one here cared that the bars were supposed to be smoke free facilities now. A large mahogany bar ran from left to right. Several pool tables were placed strategically throughout, and the only addition to the bar was an assortment of video gambling machines. The Family still kept an office in the back to conduct business when needed, but more often than not, business meetings were handled elsewhere.

The café where Mr. Gambini liked to eat his meals had also remained open, mainly thanks to the sentimental value of his Family. To this day, men sat out front sipping on strong chicory coffee while watching the street lined with cars and sidewalk bustling with people. The café still had a heavy

Italian flare. The bistro tables outside each had an umbrella with the name of the café imprinted on it. On the inside, the atmosphere was cozy. White tablecloths adorned each table with a candle in the center. The interior was kept dark and the main light came from an exquisite chandelier that hung in the middle of the restaurant.

Whenever he entered the café, Dominic, the present day Boss, envisioned Mr. Gambini sitting at a back table smoking a cigar and carrying on a business meeting. He had seen pictures of Mr. Gambini sitting at a far back table and even then he was an imposing man. His jet black hair was always slicked back in the photos, and his dark eyes appeared to stare right through you.

The poker room in the back was still used to this day. Whenever you entered the back room, you never knew who would participate in the poker game. It could be a prominent lawyer, doctor, politician, judge or other businessman. They came to blow off steam. Several of the more prominent people that played here had a brass nameplate to hold their seat. As a person passed away and their seat was vacated, the nameplate was moved to the wall of honor out of respect. Another wall showed the names of those who did not fulfill their debts. A code of silence was implemented for this room, and none of the names on the walls or table were to be spoken outside of this room. To do so meant permanent removal from the game.

Now, if one of these prominent businessmen or women was unable to pay their gambling debt, then they were treated the same as one of the local business owners that couldn't pay. After all, the Family didn't get where they were by turning the other cheek for anyone.

The St. Germaine Family Ten Commandments

When you join the St. Germaine Family you swear to uphold the following commandments – or your flesh will burn.

1) Never betray the Family

2) Once in the Family, it's for Life.

3) You live for the Family - The Boss is the Family.

4) Do not lie to the Family.

5) Do not steal from the Family

6) Never look at the wives of the Family.

7) Enemies are good one way - Dead.

8) Never introduce yourself to another family member.

9) Never be seen with the Badges.

10) You do not do business with other families.

Prologue

Lightning flashed overhead, illuminating the night sky as dark rain clouds hung low and threatened to release a downpour at any moment. Thunder rolled across the land as another strike of lightning streaked across the sky. The moss covered cypress trees that lined the black murky swamp water appeared ghostly in the eerie night.

The thunder helped to drown out the chanting that echoed through the night air. He watched with little interest as the voodoo priestess began her ritual. She would soon perform Vodoun, a dance ritual where the spirits came to possess the believer. At first, the rituals fascinated him, but he had since grown tired of the process. He just wanted results.

Torches illuminated the area as the drummers in the batri played relentlessly. Their incessant beating filled the night air. The costumed dancers each draped a snake over their body as they vigorously danced and gyrated around a fire as flames leapt high into the night sky. The lavender tinted smoke from the peristil fire clung to everything. As the heady scent of the eucalyptus burned his nose, an uneasiness came over him. He finally had what he wanted, and yet, it wasn't enough.

Sweat trickled down the captive's body as he desperately struggled to free himself from the bonds that restrained his ankles and wrists tightly. The voodoo priestess approached him with slow deliberation and uttered a strange language directly toward him. He watched, frozen in fear, as she opened a small pouch and poured out a yellowish brown powder into her hand. She blew the powder into his face, and he immediately started to cough. The powder coated his throat and lungs as it numbed his body. He tried to free himself from the restraints once more, but his body refused to respond.

As the voodoo priestess moved closer to him, he watched in terror as she reached into his chest and grabbed at his beating heart. This couldn't be happening. It had to be a nightmare.

The man who ordered this turned away in disinterest.

Chapter 1

New Orleans 1870

A young boy of nine sat in his makeshift bedroom and listened intently to his parents' conversation. If his dad found him eavesdropping, he would whoop him good. While listening to what they were saying, he mindlessly took his index finger and toyed with the rapidly expanding hole in his threadbare pajamas.

They came to America for a better life, but they had yet to find it. His parents had the same problems here as they did in France. This was supposed to be the land of the free, but there were just as many rules here as back home. Back home, he knew how to earn spare money to help his parents put food on the table, but he had not found that here. He knew nothing of this new country, but tomorrow morning he would find a way to help his parents. He was tired of going to bed hungry, listening to his parents fight and his mom crying herself to sleep. His dad tried hard, but there were too many people here and not enough work to go around.

When he heard his name he cringed, knowing that they were not fighting about the lack of money, but their son. He was sent home from school with a note again. He saw the disappointment in his momma's eyes when he handed her the note. The fight had not been his fault, this time. The older boys were picking on a peeshwank (a small child) in school. The little boy didn't even stand up to the bullies. Instead, he sat there crying, curled up in a ball. Mais non, he wouldn't stand for that one bit. Those boys got what they deserved. His dad may scold him for not controlling his temper, but at least those kids wouldn't pick on the peeshwank again.

His mother begged him to be a good boy, but there was something inside of him that he couldn't control. When he felt the anger inside of him building, he knew it would consume him. There were times like today, though, when he didn't want to control it.

When he arrived at school the next day, he noticed an extremely intimidating man waiting with one of the bullies in front of the school. He had never seen someone who even dressed like him. He must have a really important job because he wore a suit like his dad wore only to funerals back home. When they left France, his dad didn't even bother to bring it with him - saying that there would be no one to impress here. Besides, they needed the money to help pay their way over here.

The young boy took a step back and searched for another way around. He froze when he saw the bully point a finger in his direction. The neatly dressed man motioned for him to come over. Dragging his feet, he slowly walked over to them. Now he wished he had skipped school today, but his parents would have nothing of it. He had been grateful that his dad didn't scold him. His dad said he understood why he did it, but next time to please use his words rather than his fists to settle an argument.

Instead of looking up at the man, he kicked at the dirt and asked, "Am I in trouble, sir?"

The man glared down at the young boy, "Did you beat up my nephew yesterday?"

He exclaimed, "He was picking on a peeshwank and should have known better!"

The man scratched his head and asked, "What is a peeshwank?"

"They were beating up on a small boy while he just sat on the ground and cried the whole time."

Suddenly the man hit the bully behind the head and spoke a line of words he didn't understand. "I'm sorry that my nephew did that. You are a brave little boy, unlike my nephew here. I am afraid he is destined to be nothing but trouble."

He shifted his eyes from the intimidating man to the bully, unsure of what to do or say. The man told him, "My nephew thinks the only way to earn respect is by being a thug. Well, I won't stand for it. How can I repay you for standing up to my nephew and protecting that little peeshwank as you say?"

He looked the man directly in the eyes, and told him, "I need a job sir. Mais, no one wants to give me an odd job; they think I am a babe. I ain't no babe and can work just as hard as the men they hire."

He let out a laugh, "If you want a job, then I will give you a job. Meet me here after school and I will show you where to come to work, okay? But if I give you a job, you can't tell anyone, okay? Not even your parents."

"Mais oui. Yes, sir."

The day seemed to drag on. He was ready for school to be over so that he could start his new job. The man never did say what he would pay him, but anything was better than nothing.

As soon as he burst through the doors leading outside, he saw the man who promised him a job. He patted the young boy on the back, "Are you ready to get to work."

"Mais oui."

"Okay, I am going to show you where you will come every afternoon after school. Remember, you can tell no one of this."

"Mais oui. I am thankful to have a job, sir."

He laughed, "Such troubles for one so young."

As soon as he entered the man's office, he knew this man was rich. The lights on the ceiling sparkled like the stars in the sky. The man caught him looking up in awe and laughed, "That is a crystal chandelier."

"I have never seen anything so beautiful."

He pushed the young boy along, "Come on, we still have much to do."

He was excited and intimidated at the same time to be in a place this extravagant. He felt out of place and was afraid to touch anything. If only he could tell his Mere everything that he saw today. She wouldn't believe him, though. She would think he was making up tall tales to make her laugh. Today, though, was the day that would change his future forever.

***

The little French boy's legs pedaled the sleek new bicycle as fast as he could down the bumpy, cobblestoned streets of the French Quarter. He had never owned anything as nice as the gift from his new boss and took extreme pride in the bike, being mindful to avoid the water puddles on the road.

The bike had been a bonus for working so hard this last month. It took him several days to learn how to ride the bike, but now that he had the hang of it, he could do his errands faster. Especially one as far away as this errand. Plus, on the bike he didn't worry about the soles of his shoes melting on the hot sidewalks. He wished he could take his new gift home, but that would bring questions he couldn't answer. Besides, he didn't want his parents to feel guilty that they couldn't afford a gift as nice as this. No, it was best that he kept the bike at work. His new boss understood when he explained the reasoning behind it.   In fact, Mr. Gambini may respect him more for that decision.

He may only be a nine year old boy, but his life made him grow up faster than the other kids in his class. While others rushed out of school to go and play before going home to do their chores, he rushed out the door to his job. Not that he hated working and helping his family, but he occasionally wondered what his life would be like if he didn't have the worries that he had. What would it be like to always have food on the table and a warm bed to sleep in? He learned that problems had solutions, and sometimes the solutions were too difficult to make happen. However, he was determined to help his parents out. When he looked at his mother, he saw the worry in her eyes. He could feel the weight of his dad's worries on his shoulders. He wasn't sure if he ever wanted to grow up and experience the kind of pain they had in their grown up lives. At his young age, he already had problems with handling the trials that life threw his way. He could just imagine how much harder his life would be as he aged. Mais non, his childhood may not be as happy as his friends, but he was grateful to have a roof over his head and a job that helped put food on the table.

The young boy sometimes worried that his parents would be disappointed in him if they ever found out who he worked for. His Dad believed in honest work. Although the young boy didn't know exactly what his new boss did, he doubted the work was on the up and up. Especially since his boss stressed to be careful if the police asked him why he was in this area. He once overheard Mr. Gambini explain to a man that no one would stop a young boy delivering a package, but if one of his men were noticed, the police would definitely stop the man.

When Mr. Gambini handed him the package earlier, he told him to guard it as if his life depended on it and to give it to no one other than whom he was supposed to. If the man wasn't there, he must wait for him and not return until he delivered the package. He wasn't sure exactly what it was, but the newspaper smelled like the docks. He swore that a fish was wrapped in the newspaper, but that couldn't be. Why would the police want to stop someone delivering a fish? But he didn't want to disappoint Mr. Gambini, especially not after he had been so nice to him and treated him well. Sometimes Mr. Gambini would give him a nice piece of meat or even fresh milk or eggs to bring home to his momma. Whenever she asked how he came across the food, he explained how he did an odd job for the butcher or someone else. Instead of money they repaid him in goods that would just be thrown away. She then kissed him on the head and told him how thoughtful he was to help his Mere and Pere the way he did. At first, he felt guilty lying to them, but lying was better than seeing the disappointment in their eyes.

After he had delivered the package to the store owner, he maneuvered his bike towards the levee road. He wanted to catch a fish or two for supper. It had been a while since he went fishing on the river and fish sounded ideal for dinner. He could already see the smile on his momma's face when he brought her a mess of fish all nicely cleaned for her to cook.

The bank of the river had hardened and smoothed out over the years. It had become a firm mud. He hid his bike in some bushes on the embankment and walked the rest of the way. He didn't want to get his bike dirty, and he doubted it would be easy to pedal in this mud.

As he made his way to his fishing spot, he fashioned himself a bamboo pole to use. His dad taught him this soon after moving here. There was always something sturdy around to use for a pole, and he kept a pouch with a knife, string and hook in his pocket for just this occasion.

It took him no time to finish the pole and throw the line in the water. As he waited for a fish to bite, he watched the sun glisten off the rippling water. This spot was peaceful and calm. He listened to the sound of the water lapping against the river bank and relaxed as he felt the afternoon breeze against his skin. The smell that blew in off the Gulf enveloped him. He was in his own little world at the moment.

From his fishing spot, he watched as the smudge pots bobbed up and down in the water. Buoys made from old beer barrels were placed offshore to warn ships of the sandbanks nearby. As much as he missed living in France, there were times like this that he enjoyed living here. He never had views like this in France. He found the water calming. He could sit here, fish and not think about life's trials and tribulations. What would it be like to live on the river and work on a boat? Would he find the water still as calming? After this afternoon's episode with the package delivery, he needed some peace and quiet. He didn't understand why the old man had become angry about the package. The old man screamed and yelled at him as if he were a piece of white trash. He hoped Mr. Gambini asked him how it went so he could tell him not to deal with that cranky old man again. There had to be someone else he could do business with.

As the sun went down, he gathered the day's catch and went back home. Some shady characters preferred to sleep here, so he had to leave before dark. His dad warned him about the problems that occurred down here at night, and he didn't want to be near that kind of trouble.

After he had dropped off his bike, he made his way back to their tiny apartment. When he rounded one corner, a man stepped from the shadows and waved at the young boy as he passed.

One day, he would stop and talk to the elderly man. He would ask him why he lived on the streets and didn't have a house. Although if he stopped to think about it, what they lived in was barely a house. The apartment was small and drafty, but at least it kept the rain off of their heads and provided a place to sleep safely at night.

As he neared Mr. Rampart's garden, he slowed to see if he found any tomatoes or other goodies his mom could use with supper. On one bush, he saw several ripe tomatoes and the biggest bell pepper he'd ever seen.

He knocked on Mr. Rampart's door. Mr. Rampart grumpily opened the door, "What do you want, boy?"

Looking the man directly in the eye, he said, "May I trade you a fish for something from your garden."

"Mais, you say you have a fish?"

"Mais oui. A nice sized one too."

***

Mr. Rampart looked at the young boy's catch and smiled. He didn't want to break the boy's heart by telling him he could catch his own fish. Besides, he was merely trying to help out his parents. He had seen the young boy talking with Mr. Gambini and thought of warning him about the man, but decided against it. Mais non, he didn't want to even think of that man's name because it would bring him trouble. If the young boy kept associating with that man, he would speak with the boy's dad. Gambini was the last man anyone on this street, or this town, should talk to.

He told the young boy, "Leave me one of the smaller fish and go get you a few things from the garden, but leave me something to fix my supper with, you hear?"

***

"Mais oui." He responded as he ran off to the garden before he changed his mind. He already knew what he wanted. With the tomatoes and bell pepper his momma could make her coubion. He had seen her make it enough times to know she needed tomatoes, bell pepper and onions for the gravy. Luckily, Mr. Rampart had all three in his garden. He could already smell the fish cooking.

He burst through the door to find his mom at the kitchen sink, "Momma, look what I got for supper."

She looked at her son's smile and asked, "Mais, what did you bring for supper, cher?"

He dropped his treasures in the kitchen sink and listened to his mother's gasp, "Mon Dieu, what pretty fish! Is that what kept you from coming straight home today?"

Smiling broadly, "Oui, momma. I wanted to get you something special for tonight. It has been a long time since I went fishing. Don't worry, I was very careful. I even stopped by Mr. Rampart's and traded a fish for everything to fix your coubion."

She ruffled his hair, "Why, aren't you getting to be a resourceful little boy?"

He puffed out his chest, "I ain't a little boy anymore, Momma. I can help out around here."

Holding back the tears, she informed him, "You are turning into a fine young man, my son."

He looked at her with pride in his eyes and hoped she was telling the truth. Would she be disappointed if he told her who he worked for in the afternoon? He had heard people whisper that the man was in the Mafia, but he wasn't sure what that meant. He could ask his dad, but then that would lead to questions he could not answer. Besides, Mr. Gambini was good to him and he enjoyed working for him.

***

While he listened to his family sleep, he thought about how the day had played out. The day started out as it always did, but somewhere along the way it went drastically wrong. How had his life come to this? He came here to find a better life, and he had let them down. He found it hard to look at himself in the mirror nowadays.

If he hadn't gone earlier than usual to pick up the daily delivery from the shop owner, then he wouldn't have witnessed the man being murdered. Now, what was he to do? How could he protect his family? They barely had enough money to survive on, much less move from here.

Even if they moved, where would they go? They couldn't go back home. If he did, he would surely be imprisoned. He tried to make an honest living here, but he was tempted to slip back to his old ways.

Perhaps he could work something out with this mafia family. Maybe if they knew about his special skills, he could find work within The Family and it would save him from the same fate as that shop owner.

Being a contract killer didn't bother him. He saw death as a reward, one where a person could leave behind all the pain that life entailed. This world had too much disease and hardship. A person could only endure so much and death was merely an end to the suffering.

From the outside, he didn't have the look of an ice cold killer. He loved his family and strived to be a loving and gentle father. He was fortunate to be blessed with such a loving wife and healthy child.

He should have kept to the trade he knew best when arriving here. Then perhaps they wouldn't be living in this dump. At least their apartment was on the second floor. When building this city, no one took into consideration that this area was below sea level.

Where they lived flooded easily. The neighbors living on the first floor were forced to move to higher ground when the rains really came down. The few times when they had to relocate, there was a little church near the French Quarter that allowed them to stay until the water receded.

This land was nothing like his homeland; it was untamed, wild and beautiful. There were towering cypress trees and massive oak trees that dripped with moss which swayed in the wind. The sweetest smelling flowers bloomed here and filled the night air with their fragrant scents. When the town was dark and all was quiet, he could hear the noises that came from the river. He found those sounds relaxing.

This small apartment may not be much, but at least it was a roof over their heads. If he found a better paying job, they could move out of this place. He'd heard that there were back breaking jobs working the fields on the plantations. They even paid the women and children to work there. However, he would not permit his wife to work in the fields. He knew her, though, and if needed she would go to work without uttering a single complaint. Right now, she ironed for women who spent their husband's hard earned money rather than iron themselves. At least it was honest work and helped make the ends meet.

Chapter 2

The Mafia Prince - Present Day

Currently, there were two powerful mafia families vying for control and one smaller family that was fast on its way to causing problems for them. He, however, had been born into one of the most powerful families here in New Orleans, Louisiana. His Family was comprised of a rich background in power and traditions. It had always been an intricate network of businesses, legal and otherwise, along with old money and a few Italian beliefs added in for good measure.

While each mafia family had claimed a territory where it operated its rackets, his Family had grown to include most of New Orleans and several small towns throughout Louisiana, Mississippi, and Texas. They were working on including Florida as well.

However, if the Mafia Prince had his way, his Family would soon become one of the largest crime families of the underworld. Over the past few decades, their power had been strengthening and he wanted it to continue to grow. He planned to take over most, if not all, of the United States.

Growing up, his father made sure that as the eldest son, he knew the Family business well. He had been reminded numerous times that he was the Mafia Prince and was taught the intricacies involved with the business.

His father had placed a lot of expectations on him. By the age of ten, he'd earned a black belt in martial arts and could throw a punch just like an adult.

When he was around nine years old, his dad caught him using one of his younger brothers as a punching bag. The

Mafia Prince figured his dad would beat his ass. Instead, he gave him a lesson on the proper way to hit.

"Son, you hit like a girl. No son of mine will ever hit like a girl. First, you never hit someone with your fist closed. When you hit with your fist closed, you may break or dislocate your wrist. You always hit with the palm of your hand. That way you exert more force and are less likely to break your wrist."

His father took his hand in his and showed him the correct way to hit. He continued to practice hitting his father until he had the hang of it.

Patting him on his back, his father told him, "That's good. Now I want to teach you about pressure points." His father taught him where the pressure points were on the neck, back of the head, arms, torso, legs and even the groin. "Now the important thing is," his father informed him, "not to squeeze with just your hands, you must also use your arm muscles. You want to disrupt the blood flow in the vein. Once you achieve that, you have about five minutes before they pass out, longer than that and you risk the chance of killing that person. Now, if you wish to kill a person, then by all means keep going."

His dad then placed his hands on the base of his neck, "Now you remember that pressure point on the back of your head that I told you about?"

"Yes, sir."

"Well, the most important thing to remember is if you hit someone there hard enough, you can kill him instantly, but you must remember that it is right at the base of the skull. That is also where you want to break someone's neck. Again, that will kill them instantly, but more importantly, if you do it wrong, then you will only paralyze the person. If the person lives, they may rat you out. You never want to leave behind witnesses, you understand?"

"Yes, sir."

"If someone ever grabs you and tries to break your neck or for anything else, remember to let yourself go completely slack. If you do this, the person will have to hold onto your full weight and won't be able to concentrate on breaking your neck. When you hit the ground don't get back up, instead use the closest foot to your assailant and kick him in the knee as hard as you can."

For his sixteenth birthday, he received a brand new red Corvette and a knife. His mother shook her head and walked away. His father once again took him outside and explained how to use it. "Now that you are moving up in the business, it is time you know how to use a knife. With this knife, you will be able to disable someone or kill them." From there, his father showed him where to kill a man or bring him excruciating pain. They spent almost three hours outside playing with the knife and the correct way to hold it. He was also taught that when you stabbed a man you must twist the knife a good complete turn before removing it. It ensured that the wound remained open. Where most fathers taught their sons how to throw a ball or some other nonsense, his father taught him how to fight and kill a man without leaving a mark on him. He learned to enjoy the feel of killing someone and watching the life leave a body.

Sometimes he missed a day of school when his father had a job he deemed more important. He was forbidden to participate in after school activities. Instead, his father saved certain jobs until the end of school rather than leaving them for someone else in the Family to handle.

His father liked to brag that his son was one hell of a Mafia Prince, and that he soaked up information like a sponge. He never forgot what he was taught, ever. Along with how to kill someone or cause them extreme pain, he was taught how to handle pain.

Growing up, his mother insisted that he go to church every Sunday and attend religious classes without fail. She also made sure he understood the importance of confession and how it was good for the soul. Being a devout Roman Catholic, his mother believed without confession he would never make it into heaven. So with that understanding, it was mandatory that he and his father go to confession every Sunday before church. His father had paid the church dearly to forgive his confessions.

As he learned more about the family business, his dad allowed him to watch the cleaner at work. Beforehand, his dad emphasized the importance of never divulging the cleaner's identity. Even his underboss did not know the cleaner's identity. While members of the Family carried out most clips, the cleaner was used for specific hits. The Family never recruited an outsider for any job, especially a clip, and witnesses were quickly eliminated.

He had watched as the cleaner took the body out of the trunk and placed it on a piece of plastic previously laid down. His movements were quick, fluid and done with extreme efficiency, never showing any emotion. The cleaner's masterful performance proved his experience and strength. Now, the Mafia Prince understood why his dad called this man. Before throwing the body parts in the river, he picked up a bottle and poured acid over the body. As soon as it hit the body a sizzling noise sounded. This step removed any fingerprints and trace evidence before disposal.

His father proudly told everyone that his son had natural born instincts for this business. Those instincts could not be taught, and how someone born with that gift would go far in this business. When the time came for him to take over, he could handle it.

As time passed, he learned the importance of controlling his anger, and, when necessary, to turn away from temptation and contain his passion. At the age of eighteen, there was not a weapon he didn't know how to use. He could use knives, guns and his hands to kill a person. He also learned the importance of interrogation. He knew how to use something as simple as water to have a man begging for his life and talking as if his life depended on it, which in most cases it did. By the time he graduated high school, he had seen and done it all. He could watch some of the most hideous things and be numb to it all. He could kill a man and then turn around and eat a steak dinner.

Chapter 3

As Dominic St. Germaine hurried around, already late for the day, he caught a glimpse of his great great grand-pere's picture as he walked downstairs. Jacque St. Germaine had been a handsome man, and his French heritage had been clear to anyone who saw him. When he first laid eyes on Lucille Picou, he knew he had to make her his wife. The two had a whirlwind courtship and married three months after meeting. He liked to tell everyone that his southern-bred, debutante wife had married up in the world. Their love story was told from generation to generation, and it was one he never grew tired of hearing. It meant that true love existed.

Within their first year of marriage, the eldest son was born. Right after the birth of his son, he moved his growing family into a sprawling estate that became known as the St. Germaine Plantation. It was more of a mansion really; Jacque St. Germaine made sure that the expansive grounds were kept immaculate. Jacque wanted to flaunt that business was thriving, and life was good. There were those in town that had labeled him river trash. If only his parents had lived to see their son make something of his life.

Anyone could see the pride in Jacque St. Germaine's eyes whenever he mentioned how well his new hotel, Maison de St. Germaine, was doing. He especially loved to rub it in his biggest competition's face, Henri Scarcelli. Everyone knew that the Scarcelli Family was from an old Italian Family, meaning they were mafia. Jacques St. Germaine wasn't afraid of Scarcelli and made sure that his business flourished in spite of Scarcelli and his threats.

Even after Jacque St. Germaine moved his family to the plantation, he kept the penthouse free for when he needed to stay in town for a meeting, or to cavort with a comare (mistress) or two. Jacque loved his new wife deeply, but he had a wandering eye and figured as long as his wife didn't know what he did behind her back, they were okay.

The St. Germaine empire grew with his great great grand-pere's good head for business. Jacque St. Germaine's eldest son, Jean Paul St. Germaine, wanted to venture out into construction. But Jacque stressed that the Scarcelli Family was too deeply entangled with the construction business and that they should leave it be. After Jacque's passing, Jean Paul ventured into the construction business, doing it slow and steady as to not cause waves with the Scarcelli Family. So by the time Dominic's grandfather, Jean Paul Jr., came along, the St. Germaine Family business had grown at an expeditious pace. Maison de St. Germaine, was always booked, and their construction business was booming. They were awarded several contracts for new buildings despite the Scarcelli Family threats. Jean Paul Jr. grew their business even more by opening a car dealership. There were enough Family members to help run the new business where they didn't have to bring in outsiders.

As the St. Germaine Family business grew, it caught the attention of not only the Scarcelli Family, but that of another Mafia Family vying for control of Louisiana. This other family was not Italian mafia, but one started by a Frenchman. He'd heard how well the Scarcelli Family did in their crime syndicate and figured if an Italian could do it, then a Frenchman could do it better.

Even with the constant pressure from these two mafia families, the St. Germaine Family flourished in their business ventures.

By the time Dominic made it to the office, his cellphone rang. It was his brother, Simon. "Dominic you need to come back home. Dad had a heart attack. Mom has already called the ambulance."

Dominic could hardly believe his ears, "I will meet you at the hospital. It is faster than me coming back home. Are you sure it was a heart attack?"

His brother let out a sigh, "I don't know Dom. Something isn't right about this. Dad was at the dining room table talking to Mom about what all he had to do today when he just collapsed."

Without even entering the office building, he climbed right back into this car and drove to the hospital. Once he arrived at the hospital, it seemed to take him forever to find a parking spot. No sooner than he walked into the emergency room bay doors, he saw the ambulance pull up. He watched as his mother stepped out with his dad on the gurney. His heart broke to see the tears in his mother's eyes.

Chapter 4

Dominic, his mother, and siblings climbed into the limousine that would follow the hearse to the cemetery. Dominic's mom had not stopped crying since his father passed away. The doctors confirmed that he died that morning at the breakfast table. They said it was as if his heart had just exploded. The surgical cardiologist stated his dad had more than likely suffered from an undiagnosed enlarged heart for quite some time, and it couldn't take the strain anymore. Dominic still found that hard to believe.

He looked out the window and watched as the funeral procession meandered down the streets of New Orleans. The limo followed directly behind, while the other cars followed suit.

The wrought iron gates that separated the cemetery from the rest of New Orleans were exquisite in their design. Within this cemetery were buried some of the most famous and infamous citizens of New Orleans. Death played no favorites when it came to your social status. In the end, everyone was the same, ashes to ashes and dust to dust.

This cemetery would be the final resting place of his father. Over one hundred cars lined the small roads in the cemetery. It appeared everyone wished to pay their final respects, or to possibly spit on the man's grave. Dominic wasn't sure which. His father was not a well-loved man and had many enemies. Over half of these people probably wanted to make certain that the man was buried six feet under.

As they drove up, he noticed the manager of the cemetery waiting for their arrival. One by one, the mourners emerged from their cars and somberly surrounded the family mausoleum. Chairs were set up for the family members, and there was only room for a few of the mourners inside the mausoleum.

Dominic watched as tears flowed down his mother's face. He wondered if they were from anguish, sadness or regret. His father had been a hard man, but he made sure they knew he loved them, even if he never said it. Dominic wished he had told his father that he loved him as well.

He placed an arm around his mother to help console her, "It will be all right." She buried her head in his shoulder as grief consumed her once again.

He watched as the coffin was wheeled into the tiny room overflowing with flowers. As the priest made his way to the front of the mausoleum, Dominic let his thoughts wander. He hoped that he could fill his dad's shoes. He had been the backbone of the Family and his absence would be greatly apparent.

Through heartbreaking sobs, his mom said, "I can't imagine my life without him. He was my everything!"

Dominic wondered what would happen to their tight knit family now that their dad had passed away. Would they still meet on Sundays for dinner after mass? It was the one day where work was put aside so the family could get together to laugh and swap stories. It was one of the only times he saw his dad happy.

As he gazed down at the casket, he told his father, "I promise to keep the family traditions alive and the business successful Dad. I will make those who did this pay. I will take this to the mattresses." Dominic knew that the Scarcelli Family had made good on their threats no matter what the doctor said. Somehow, they got to him, if only he could find out how.

Dominic looked around the room overflowing with mourners. As the priest spoke, the room fell silent. "Our Father, who art in heaven…"

The priest's voice resonated in the small room. Even though the room was full and his family was here, he felt alone. He wanted to scream to those around him that his father should not have been taken from them. Most of the mourners weren't concerned with his family's grief; they wanted to make certain that the man was dead.

From the back of the mausoleum, he caught a movement in the crowd and his guard immediately went up. Frankie and Alfonso Scarcelli walked into the mausoleum as if they owned the place and Dominic saw red. How dare these men come here!

Dominic forced himself to ignore the Scarcellis and brought his attention back to the funeral. The funeral was a solemn, unifying ritual that reminded Dominic how short life was.

After the funeral, several of the mourners met back at the house. Everyone had a story to tell about his father. Some stories were about how kind his dad had been to them and how he had helped them out in a time of need. As each story continued, they held Dominic's attention. He never knew his dad had done some of these great things and he was amazed at his father's generosity and compassion for these people. He always considered his dad to be strictly interested in money and nothing else. Now, he knew better; unfortunately, it was after he was dead and buried.

After the guests departed, Dominic walked into his dad's office. He had been in this room numerous times, but he felt as if he was invading his father's space today. There were so many memories in here and now this office, this business, was his. He had some big shoes to fill.

He spotted the decanter of scotch and the humidor near his dad's desk. If Dominic closed his eyes, he could see his dad sitting at his desk with a tumbler of scotch and smoking his Cohiba cigar. Several newspapers remained scattered about the office just as his dad had left everything.

A gnawing feeling began somewhere in his heart and worked its way to his gut. If only he could have saved his dad. They'd assumed he was untouchable, but they were wrong.

Dominic poured himself a tumbler of scotch and walked around the office as he gathered his thoughts. He grew up in this house, but now he felt like an intruder. He found it difficult to believe that his dad would no longer walk through those doors.

No longer would his dad take his mom out to their favorite restaurants or grumble about escorting her to the opera. His Dad had no more society soirees to attend or business meetings to oversee. He didn't need to worry about his enemies, constantly wondering if the other Mafia Family would finally make good on their threats.

As Dominic made his way into the family room, he caught a glimpse of the family photos and walked over to where they were proudly displayed. His father never liked having his picture taken so there were very few pictures memorializing him; however, his dad made sure he had pictures and videos of his children's lives.

The rest of his siblings looked like his father; however, Dominic had more of a resemblance to his mother.

Dominic's dad constantly jested that if his mother had been a boy she would have looked just like Dominic. Dominic inherited his temper and business sense from his dad though.

He couldn't believe how much his life had changed in the blink of an eye. Soon, he would be twenty-one, yet he felt as if he was already thirty. Not only would he marry soon, but now he was also head of the Family. A lot of people counted on him, and he didn't want to disappoint anyone.

Chapter 5

Mariam Honore closed her eyes and remembered what an inquisitive little girl her granddaughter had been. As Bianca grew into a budding young woman, Mariam ignored the warning signs emanating from Bianca.

Her heart broke when Bianca moved to New York, and she prayed to the gods that Bianca would not pursue her desires there. As she neared seventy, though, she could no longer ignore what she had feared. She sensed her granddaughter's powers strengthening and it was time to bring her back home, away from those people and that way of life. It may be the only way to save her.

Lately, she had such intense feelings about her granddaughter and the evil that seemed to lurk near her. As she stared out the kitchen window, she fixated spellbound on the moon hanging in the night sky. A red haze surrounded the moon, which meant that her time was running out. What concerned her most was that under the red haze was a twisted and snarled double halo. Many years ago, her grand-mere explained the signs of the moon. A halo around the moon meant a change was in the future. A double halo was never good; especially, a double halo entangled and snarled. Somewhere a love affair had gone wrong and anything could happen in the near future. This was when you should not answer your phone or see who was knocking at your door. For those who knew what the signs of the moon meant, they knew to keep their doors and windows locked; however, trouble always came unannounced and took over before you knew what had hit you.

Seeing the moon in its present appearance sent a shiver down her spine. It was almost as if a snake was looping itself around the full moon twice before settling in. It was an omen. She wondered how many more people were staring at the moon and saw the same thing. It wasn't an illusion, and while some considered it mystical, this moon worried her. Nights like this when the air was warm and the sky as black as ink and just as thick, a single noise could be swallowed up and never heard. This was when the devil was afoot - waiting to see what trouble he could cause. If she breathed in the night air, she could almost smell the sulfurous odor of trouble.

She feared that trouble was in store for her granddaughter at this very moment. Was the devil lurking about, waiting to lure her into his treachery? Calling Bianca home may be the only way to stop the chain of events she had foreseen from unfolding. She couldn't bear the thought that her own flesh and blood may practice black magic. Voodoo was intended to be used for good and not evil. She had taught Bianca better than that.

She shook her head. Was it because death was so near that she felt such deep regret? Why was it only now that she feared what was to become of her granddaughter? She could have called her back at any time, but why had she chosen now to summon her home. Surely she didn't secretly want her to learn black magic? Those questions had been plaguing her mind over the last few days. Her passing would not have any effect on her family, but it may tempt Bianca to delve further into black magic. What she dreaded most were the revelations from last night's dream. She prayed to the gods that she had time to change what she had foreseen. If that change did not take place, the world everyone knew would soon crumble. That weighed heavy on her shoulders.

If only Bianca had the same inner strength as she had to turn away from the callings of the black magic. Oh yes, it had called her when she was younger, but she found the integrity to renounce the temptations. However, she feared that Bianca had not pulled away from those same temptations. She worried that Bianca did not use sound judgment when it came to evil. Her granddaughter had intuitive abilities and had the makings of becoming a great voodoo priestess. Even at a young age, Bianca embraced the voodoo religion and absorbed everything she was taught.

She wished her daughter had embraced the voodoo religion as well as her granddaughter, but she did not believe in the religion like Bianca. No, Bianca was special; they were kindred spirits. She knew that as soon as she was born. Her daughter questioned everything about the religion, but her granddaughter treated the religion with the love and respect that it deserved. Voodoo was not something to play around with. Only those who truly believed in it could make it work, and right now she hoped that Bianca followed the correct path in life. Either way, her granddaughter's life was soon to change forever.

Mariam knew her time was near. She heard the death watch beetle ticking. She wanted Bianca home so that she could change her ways before the future became written in stone. She prayed that the fate she had seen in her dreams was not guaranteed. No matter how hard she tried to intervene, it seemed that fate would fulfill its destiny, and thus had her fearing for Bianca.

Chapter 6

Bianca Honore's family had had mixed religions for generations now. She had been named after the reigning Queen of New Orleans voodoo since 1983.

Voodoo came to New Orleans with the influx of West African slaves who escaped Haiti. Louisiana Voodoo was a mix of African and Caribbean Voudou. Christianity, more specifically Catholicism, was thrown in the religion as well. It had been a way of life for decades now, not only by the African Americans but the whites as well. Even the Hispanics practiced the voodoo religion.

Her grand-mere was a traditional high priestess here. People sought out her grand-mere secretly for various cures and specific blessings. Bianca learned the ways of voodoo and Santeria from a young age. Over the years, she became familiar with rare New Orleans original voodoo occult items along with how to make magical fetishes, small voodoo statues and good luck charms. Her specialty was Gris Gris bags and voodoo dolls.

Like her grand-mere, she was fluent in both voodoo and hoodoo. Voodoo was a religion; hoodoo was the side that dealt with hexes and such. Some around here considered those that practiced hoodoo as witches, which was ridiculous. It had been that way for over a century and there was no changing that, as much as she would like to. Her grand-mere always talked openly about the racism she grew up with coming from a voodoo family. If anything bad happened, it was blamed on the voodoo woman; she must have put a curse on you. Any hint of misfortune had people pointing fingers. Her grand-mere prayed to the gods that things would change by the time Bianca grew up, but it

hadn't. She was constantly teased about being related to
the voodoo witch; children were warned that if Bianca did
not like something they did she would put a hex on them.
It still hurt today when she remembered how cruel people
had been.

Growing up had not been pleasant. She never had friends.
The other children avoided her like the plague. Throughout
school, she ate her lunch alone in the cafeteria; everyone
was too afraid to even sit by her. If she touched a pencil, no
other student dared touch it; fearing she'd put a spell on it.
Even though Bianca excelled in sports and school work, she
was picked last for any team choices during physical
education class or even in the school classroom. She never
received invitations to parties or outings; she was treated as
an outcast. She always dreamed of being invited to
sleepovers, but she was always left out. The teachers never
reprimanded students for being mean; they could be just as
cruel, if not crueler.

When the other students made snide comments or rude
noises behind her back, she swore one day she would make
them regret being mean to her. At times, they were so
cruel that Bianca couldn't resist muttering to herself,
spinning in circles and pointing her finger at whoever teased
her ruthlessly at the time. She laughed when they ran away
from her in tears and hollering that the crazy girl had put a
hex on them. She added to the persona by dressing in
black; lurking in the shadows and sitting in the back of the
classroom until the day was over, but never once did she
raise her hand in class. All through school, no one really
knew what special talents she kept well hidden.

Her illusion of being a black magic practitioner was
personified when the stray black cats in town followed her
to and from school every day. Wherever she went, they

followed. Now, contrary to popular belief, black cats brought good luck, not bad. Black cats made people jittery and scared. She found the fact that black cats were scary hilarious. They were the most loving of the cats, always wanting to be spoiled. Unfortunately, some people in town believed that the black cats were her familiars, animals that she used to do her evil bidding. It was rumored that the more familiars a person had, the nastier the bidding would be and she had at least a dozen black cats that followed her. The reason they followed her could have something to do with the fact that she carried tuna fish with her everywhere she went. After all, she needed something to feed the stray cats. They couldn't possibly find enough food to fill their tummies on the streets.

No matter what nasty rumors these kids spread, Bianca knew their dirty little family secrets. Those same kids who were mean to her had parents who sought out her grand-mere for charms and potions. She knew when Mike Savoie's dad was cheating on his mom because his mom came looking for a potion to make him pay for his infidelity. So when she wanted to get even, she would let it slip out at the most inopportune times.

Even her grand-mere was never invited to social functions, but when they had a child sick to his stomach or a headache that wouldn't go away, they sought her out before old Dr. Thomas Guillory. Women sought her grand-mere out when they had matters of the heart that needed to be tended to as well. It was not unusual to hear a knock at the back door at the stroke of midnight because the person didn't want to be seen using the front door. Bianca found it funny how when someone wanted something bad enough, they found the courage to do something that frightened them normally. It annoyed her how fickle people could be. Until they needed something, they forgot that you even existed. It was only when they needed something that they acted as if you were their best friend.

It didn't matter to her grand-mere who they were or what they needed, as long as they paid for her services. Her grand-mere could tell from the way someone walked up to the house how desperate they were and her price increased for whatever service they needed. Yes, her grand-mere was indeed a shrewd business woman. Her grand-mere enjoyed practicing her voodoo and swore that was how she remained young. Bianca firmly believed that statement too; her grand-mere never looked a day over thirty to her. Bianca wasn't sure of her grand-mere's exact age, but her momma had been in her twenties when she had been born. So her grand-mere had to be close to her forties when she was born.

Bianca was a light sleeper and listened for the sound of people knocking at the back door. She would quietly get out of bed, tiptoe to her hiding spot and watch as her grand-mere performed her rituals for those people. From her hiding spot, she learned what each person desired the most. She learned at an early age that love made a person do desperate things. That desire for another individual could control every part of you. Bianca learned how to control her passions and never allowed her passions to be ruled by another.

She learned that sometimes getting what your heart desired could be very dangerous, if not deadly. Once a curse was performed; there was no taking it back. If you truly wanted that person to love you until the end of time, you better be certain that was really what you wanted.

Having a boyfriend growing up was out of the question. Most of the boys were afraid if they so much as touched her, their peckers would fall off. Bianca sometimes wondered if that had been her grand-mere's doing more than anything else. She regularly warned Bianca to stay away from them boys; that they were after only one thing and nothing else.

The only time she felt normal was at home with her grand-mere. Bianca's momma had better things to do than tend to a child; she wanted nothing to do with the voodoo religion that her momma practiced, and she wanted to forget about her horrid childhood. She spent most of her time in Baton Rouge, where no one knew of her momma's family.

By the time Bianca turned eighteen, she'd had enough of this town and the small minded people here. She wanted a real life, one where she could be herself. She was ready to spread her wings and not be looked upon as a freak. Perhaps she did take after her momma in some ways. She wanted to go where no one knew her name or her family.

Now, her grand-mere was calling her back home to take over the family business. She should have argued that wasn't the life she wanted, but she couldn't. Lately, she'd felt New Orleans calling out to her once again. Could it be that her destiny was waiting for her back in New Orleans?

She had mixed feelings about returning home. Her family would welcome her back with loving arms and heart warming smiles, but she felt something dark and brooding was calling her back. She was unsure of what the future held for her, but she knew she must return home.

Her grand-mere had been visiting often in her dreams, insisting that Bianca return home. She could no longer put it off. It was time to go home and face whatever fate had planned for her. She should dread returning home due to her grand-mere's declining health, but even after her grand-mere died, she would be able to talk to her.

She had a feeling there was something unfamiliar and different in store for her in the near future. This feeling should frighten her, but it didn't. She was ready to welcome whatever new changes life had to offer her.

As she neared her home, the scenery changed and reminded her how beautiful it was in New Orleans. When she reached the long stretch of bridge that brought her home, a shiver of apprehension ran down her spine. She despised this bridge, all around her was water and nothing else, but once on the other side, she would be home. It had been almost four years since she had been back, too long. On the trip home, she'd practiced her Creole since it was rusty from lack of use in New York. To stay fluent in the language she had to use it, but there were very few people in New York who understood her dialect.

The closer she got to her grand-mere, the more her stomach churned. She wondered how much her grand-mere knew about her. Could it simply be that her grand-mere wanted her home before she passed away or did she want to pull Bianca away from the life she was making for herself in New York? Of all the family left, Bianca was the only one who had an interest in the voodoo religion. The rest wanted to forget where they came from, but not her. She wanted to embrace it. This was who she was, and she was proud of it. In New York, she'd found others who welcomed her and taught her so much.

As she turned on the street her grand-mere's house was on, the rain came down in sheets. There were very few street lights here, making it difficult to see the now watery, darkened street. A shrieking wind blew past her and shook the car; Bianca wondered if this was an omen.

As the rain spattered hard against the windshield, she leaned in closer to the steering wheel to make out the road in front of her. She knew she was near when she saw the esoteric designs painted on the doors of the houses here. These signs were called veves, and they each had a purpose. Some called for assistance from the Loa, the gods of the Voodoo pantheon. There were also a few for Baron Samedi, the keeper of cemeteries and the protector of the dead. One house had a veve for Papa Legba, the chief Loa guide who interceded with the rest of the pantheon for favors. Yes, this was home. This was where she grew up and where she learned her love of voodoo.

This was where Bianca wanted to hone her skills of voodoo. She'd acquired a lot of knowledge in New York, but down here she would have the chance to become legendary. She wanted everyone to know that she could exact her revenge with voodoo. She dreamed of becoming a modern day Marie Laveau. She craved that notoriety and to use it to her advantage.

She pulled up to her grand-mere's house in the early morning hours. As soon as she stepped out of the car, the humidity of the day enveloped her. At least it was still late spring, but the summer heat would be unbearable. She had loved the cooler weather in New York. She had also met others interested in voodoo in New York and learned a lot. She learned more about the black magic, more than her grand-mere would like. Bianca always had a secret fascination with the darker aspects of voodoo. Areas that her grand-mere didn't want her to study. But Bianca's friends in New York had opened her eyes to the experience. Perhaps that was why her grand-mere called her back home; she sensed what Bianca was doing.

From the outside, the house she grew up in didn't look like much. It reminded her of a run down shack made out of old cypress. Once inside, you could see the love that was given to the house. Her grand-mere taught her that she shouldn't judge a book by its cover.

This house contained her grand-mere's most prized possessions. There were various antiques that had been passed down from generation to generation and cared for lovingly. The house was comprised of various woods from Louisiana, including the beloved cypress. There were window seats and intricate mantels all beautifully carved by her ancestors. There were dressers and tables made by hand from rosewood. There was even a special pie safe made out of a fragrant cherry wood. Even with all the knick knacks and wood in the house, you never found a hint of dust. Her grand-mere was meticulous about keeping everything spic and span. Even the wooden floors gleamed enough where she could see her reflection in the wood.

Bianca remembered how her grand-mere had kept the house dark at all times; even in the middle of the day. She had to squint to see where she was going. It helped to keep the house cool even in the hottest part of summer. By August, you would think this old house would be unbearable, but it was pleasantly comfortable. The addition of an overhead fan years ago helped to keep the air circulating in the house. Her grand-mere refused to spend money on an air conditioner, stating that if she didn't need it growing up, then she didn't need it now.

As soon as Bianca stepped into the kitchen a rush of memories assaulted her. The kitchen had not been updated in years. It had the same stove made of a heavy black metal that was installed in the 1920s. Plumbing and electricity didn't come until almost a decade later. The electricity needed to be updated badly; whenever a thunderstorm hit, the lights flickered, and you could not use a microwave in the small kitchen as the breakers were unable to handle the wattage. None of that concerned her grand-mere. As long as she could practice her spells and make her potions she was happy. The house was in need of some desperate foundation repairs. Certain areas of the floor sagged when you walked. A heavier person could fall through the weak floor in certain places. Instead of bothering with repairing those spots, her grand-mere simply moved a piece of furniture to that area to prevent someone from walking there. She shook her head at the repairs that needed to be done. It wasn't as if her grand-mere didn't have the money; it was just that she saw it as a waste of money. Why bother with the upkeep of a house that she wouldn't be living in much longer.

Chapter 7

Alfonso Scarcelli looked at his watch and grimaced. In a few hours his future wife would land in America. If he had a say in the matter, he would call off the whole thing, but his dad had stressed the importance of this union. This wedding would join two powerful families, one here in America and the other in Sicily.

Frankie Scarcelli planned on moving back to Sicily once he was comfortable leaving the business here in New Orleans under Alfonso's care. He didn't trust that his new partners in Sicily would keep him apprised of everything; he wanted to be nearby to keep an eye on things. They were venturing into several new territories that involved a lot of dough, plus they needed to make sure their cargo was kept safe.

Alfonso had heard that the other mafia families were also looking into human trafficking. It took a while for him to convince his dad that human trafficking would be profitable. Normally the Family business stayed out of smuggling goods and prostitution, but after showing his dad the numbers, he'd changed his mind. If done right, this would be very profitable. They could send the girls from Italy over here and vice versa.

If the rumors were true, it wouldn't take long for everyone to jump on this bandwagon, especially if the money were easy. The difficult thing would be kidnapping the girls and keeping them under control, but he was working on a plan for that as well. This was New Orleans after all and several people around here practiced voodoo. The key would be finding someone that practiced black magic and had no problems casting the spells he needed. It would take someone who had no regard for human life. He heard that there was also a large voodoo community in Tennessee and New York; so surely, he would find someone willing to help him.

When he asked around about voodoo priests and priestesses, he was given two names that sounded promising. One was Bianca Honore, who'd just moved back down here from New York. The other was a voodoo priestess who'd moved here from Haiti. He found a lot of research on the voodoo practiced in Haiti and it did involve black magic. What interested him was the Haitians had a way to turn the living into the walking dead.

Turning his enemies into the walking dead and having them serve as his slaves was worth considering. Just the thought of having some of his most hated enemies serving him dinner excited him. Plus, all of the labor costs that he could save by having a sweatshop run by zombies. He rubbed his hands together as his mind ran through all the possibilities. This would also keep the girls under control.

Chapter 8

Teresa Ricci waited impatiently to board the plane that would take her to her new life. No longer would she be confined to the small village near Sicily, where her parents lived in seclusion. She knew what her father did for a living, but it had never bothered her. It also didn't bother her that her future had been planned out since her birth. All she wanted was to escape this small village. Her father rarely allowed her to go into Sicily to shop or even spend the day with her friends. He had too many enemies and if something happened to her where she couldn't fulfill her destiny, then his fate could possibly be sealed as well.

Her marriage to Alfonso Scarcelli would combine two powerful families, one here in Sicily and one in America. They would be unstoppable. She heard her father talking about their future plans and she knew that they had big plans in the making.

Teresa's mom had taught her well on the importance of not asking questions when it came to The Family business. Business affairs must be kept out of their personal life. Teresa's mom may teach that, but she did not practice what she taught. Teresa's mom was a shrewd woman and Teresa had no doubt she knew everything her father did, including his numerous mistresses.

All that concerned Teresa was landing in America and finally having some freedom. She read that New Orleans was the most haunted city in America. She was disappointed to find that there wasn't much shopping to do there, but New York, San Francisco, California and other popular shopping destinations weren't far away.

As soon as she could, she planned on asking this Alfonso Scarcelli what his feelings were towards her living a life on her own. Since he had shown no desire in contacting her, she doubted he cared. The other night she did some surfing on the internet and found several pictures of the man at various functions; he was a handsome man. At least she was marrying a man she found desirable.

***

Alfonso sat in the limousine with his dad as they waited for the arrival of his future bride and in-laws. His mind went over everything he could be doing instead of waiting for a plane to arrive from Italy. His dad sent a private jet over, refusing to have his future daughter-in-law mingle with the other passengers. However, he suspected his father sent the jet because he wanted to ensure that neither the girl nor the parents changed their mind. He wanted this marriage to take place.

Alfonso was ready to get this wedding over with so that he could get back to his life. He had news for her; he refused to give up his girlfriends or current lifestyle.

His father tapped the back of his head in what he called a "love tap". In Alfonso's opinion, it was harder than needed to be considered a "love tap". His dad had yet to consider him an adult. He didn't bother taking into consideration that by the age of sixteen he'd made his bones; at the age of twenty, he'd committed more murders than possibly the cleaner. Alfonso wanted to live up to his nickname in the Family, the Mafia Prince. He didn't want anyone to think he received special treatment since he was the Boss's son.

Frankie Scarcelli looked at his son, "Your new wife is here. Let's go greet her and her family. Remember how important this union is, son."

Alfonso looked at his dad, "You have nothing to worry about, Dad. I want to join these two Mafia Families just as bad as you. We will be one of the biggest families in America and Sicily."

When Alfonso saw the Italian Princess step off the plane, his jaw dropped. She instantly stole his attention. The green dress showed her body off to perfection. She walked in stiletto heels as if she had been born to walk in them. They accentuated her shapely legs. Her glorious auburn hair cascaded down her back in luxurious waves. He wanted to lose his hands in that hair. Her body was made for sin and he could imagine the fun they would have between the sheets, and maybe out of them. Unless she was an ice princess like his mother. His mother had never been one to show affection, to her kids or her husband. He never understood why his father stayed with her.

Everything about his fiancée appeared to be flawless. Not a hair was out of place. Everything from her perfectly arched eyebrows to her manicured hands indicated that she came from a life of privilege. She was well put together and paid attention to even the smallest of details. She would make the perfect wife for a mafia prince.

From the corner of his eye, he caught a bodyguard gawking at his fiancée, and a rush of jealousy overcame him. He would teach this one the importance of breaking one of "The Ten Commandments". The man should know better than to gawk at his fiancée. Without a second thought, he took out his gun and pistol whipped the man. That would send a message out to everyone working for him not to stare at his woman; it would not be tolerated. If he had been at home, the man would have been shot, but out in the public, it would not be a wise move. The man would be dealt with later.

***

Teresa felt the intense stare from her fiancé and was taken aback when he suddenly walked over to one of his henchmen and pistol whipped him. She wasn't sure what happened, but worried that he may have a temper. She knew from experience some men believed their wife was a piece of property and treated them as such. She had seen her mom talk back to her dad, and the next morning try to hide the bruises on her body. Her mom brushed it off as part of being married to a mobster, but Teresa would not stand for that sort of thing. There were ways to deal with an abusive man and leave no marks. Her mom had been slowly poisoning her dad over these last few years. She'd recently confided to Teresa about her scheme to get rid of her abusive husband. She had been adding antifreeze to his Limoncello and various other poisons to keep him from guessing what was happening. Her father was too proud to go to the doctor with a bout of loose bowels and stomach cramps; he just said it must be the stress of his job or something he ate. She was smart enough not to poison him every day. There had been times when the man had been so mean and hateful to her that she wished to be done with it, but if he died suddenly there would be questions that she didn't want asked. Instead, when she wanted to get even with him and cause him extreme discomfort, she added a few drops of eye drops to his coffee. She explained to Teresa that you must be careful because too much could kill a person, but one or two drops kept them in the bathroom and unable to cause you any harm.

As Alfonso walked up to his fiancée, she observed him intently. For now, she would wait and see just what kind of man he was.

Chapter 9

Bianca had been home less than a month when her grand-mere passed away peacefully in the night. She came to Bianca the night she died, warning her to be careful of those she trusted and that voodoo could be dangerous in the wrong hands.

As Bianca drove to the funeral home, she wondered why her grand-mere warned her of that. She shook off the feeling and looked at everyone gathered around the entrance to the funeral home. Her grand-mere was well loved, and possibly feared, by many. Several of grand-mere's customers were happy to hear that Bianca planned to continue her grand-mere's traditions and would keep the shop open. They welcomed her in the shop; some remembered her from when she was younger. By the time her grand-mere passed away, most of her regular customers were already comfortable with Bianca performing the readings and preparing potions for them.

The number of those wishing to pass on their condolences grew rapidly as Bianca made her way into the funeral home. The wake was all day today and the actual funeral would take place tomorrow afternoon. Friends and family would also have tomorrow morning to stop by the funeral home to pay their respects. Funerals were a big deal here in South Louisiana, especially in New Orleans. This whole week had been full of tears, food and alcohol. After the funeral tomorrow, her grand-mere's life would be celebrated with a couchon de lait where everyone gathered for food, alcohol and to reminisce about her.

Years ago, her grand-mere informed her that it was Bianca's destiny to follow in her footsteps. As a child, her grand-mere taught her about voodoo and the difference between the spells. She explained to Bianca that it was in her very blood, that she had the gift. None of her other sisters had the gift, only Bianca. When Bianca asked about the black magic associated with voodoo, her grand-mere tried to deter her thought processes. Bianca wondered if her grand-mere had sensed her death approaching, or if, perhaps, she saw what Bianca was up to in New York. Could that be why she insisted Bianca come home? Bianca had felt New Orleans calling her, but she also believed that she still had more to learn in New York.   However, she could not ignore her grand-mere's request.

The next day, Bianca was amazed at how many people turned out for the funeral reception. The reception center was bursting at the seams with people. Had it not been for the fact that everyone wore black it could have easily been mistaken for a wedding reception. The parishioners must have stayed up all night cooking the food. One buffet table was piled high with various barbecued meats and side dishes. Another table overflowed with pies, cakes, cookies and other treats. Along the back wall was another table for various fruit and vegetable trays as well as an assortment of cheeses, crackers and sandwiches.

Upon entering the room, Bianca felt her grand-mere's presence. She looked around and found her in the middle of the room looking upon the crowd with a smile on her face. When she saw Bianca, she looked at her with sadness in her eyes. Bianca smiled at her grand-mere and gave her a small wave. If only she could tell her grand-mere not to worry, that everything would be okay. Bianca never could lie to her grand-mere and she would be lying if she promised that. Bianca still had no idea what her dreams meant or what the future held for her, but she intended to find out.

Chapter 10

He saw her enter the bar and was immediately mesmerized by her. She was tall, slender and had the most sensual features. They locked eyes as she made her way closer to the bar. He let his gaze roam up and down her body. He loved the way her hips swayed when she moved, it was completely erotic. This woman was an enchantress.

She wore a long tan skirt and a blood red corset top. Her voluptuous breasts looked as if they would spill free at any moment. She wore a dark brown macramé belt around her waist and her raven black hair cascaded down her back. A necklace of animal teeth and sea shells caressed her chest.

He could hardly believe it when she headed his way. It was almost as if they were magnetically drawn to each other.

****

Bianca wasn't sure what called her to this place. She just knew that she must come here tonight, now! As soon as she entered the bar, she saw him. His face was square and aristocratic. His body well defined. This man must spend a great deal of time maintaining his trim physique in the same way she did. The scent of money exuded from his pores. It was an intoxicating smell to her, one that she was familiar with. She could always spot the customers with money by the very smell when they came into her little shop. Those were the ones she could milk. She doubted this one, though, she could lure him away from his money as easily.

Unsure of what to say, he asked, "Do you come in here often?"

She shook her head side to side as she studied him intently. "Something told me to come here tonight."

Intrigued, he asked, "What is your name?"

"Bianca, Bianca Honore. I run a little voodoo shop on Bourbon Street."

***

This news had his interest piqued. Had fate brought them together? He must obtain more information about this young woman to see if she was the person he wanted to do business with. If nothing else, she may know someone he could start a business relationship with.

He asked, "So, you are from here then?"

"Mais oui. My family has lived here for generations. I moved away, but when my grand-mere's health declined, I moved back home to take over the family business."

That was why he didn't know who she was. In general, he knew all the locals, even if it was a big city. It was part of the business. In order for him to be successful, he had to know what everyone was up to. He knew what they did for a living and who they were related to in case he needed to reinforce the importance of paying him back.

"And the family business is the little voodoo shop on Bourbon Street?"

***

She nodded her head, "It is part of it. My grand-mere wanted to make sure I had not forgotten the craft before she passed away; although, if I ever have any questions, she is never far away."

Bianca could see the excitement growing in this handsome man and wondered why he was so intrigued by her family. Most people shied away when she talked about voodoo and the family business.

She smiled at him, "You never told me your name."

He bent down and whispered his name. His last name drew her attention. Everyone in New Orleans had heard of his family. They may not be the friendliest family in town, but they were loaded. She heard the family could be uppity to those they considered to be lower class. Their ancestors could be traced back to the French Acadian influx in the early 1800s. She heard rumors that they made their money by becoming bed partners with the Italian Mafia when they first set up roots here in Louisiana. So far, she hadn't been able to find anything concrete on that subject, just a lot of whispered rumors. Her grand-mere always warned her about the enforcers as she had liked to call them. They stayed away from her since she threatened them with voodoo if they set foot near her shop or her family. No one in town spoke their suspicions out loud about them. She would love to ask him if he was part of the mafia, but she didn't want to draw attention to herself.

***

By the time the Mafia Prince and his friends left the bar, it was well after two o'clock in the morning. The traffic on Bourbon Street remained heavy, except more people were inebriated than before. They had to almost shove their way through the crowd.

As they made their way to the car, he watched people as they passed. His father told him it was crucial to read someone. So he found himself always studying people.

Besides, it helped keep him sharp. He became very efficient at reading every little line on someone's face. When he read the lines on their face, he could read their story. He could tell by the way someone shifted their body if they were lying.

He learned how to pick out a badge in any crowd. He doubted the badges even knew they stuck out like a neon sign. He could tell by the expression on their face if they were a badge. They never smiled; their face had a permanent frown tattooed on it. He could also tell by their eyes. Every badge he had ever met had a tired look around their eyes.

He taught his girls how to pick out a sailor in the crowd of men on the riverfront. Those guys were easy dough. They would bring the sailors to the club for a dance and then in the back for a lay, either way they spent money on the girls and alcohol.

***

The next day when he walked into her little shop, she recognized him immediately. The sounds of Bourbon Street went silent. All that she heard was the beating of her own heart.

While she moved around the shop preparing a potion, she felt his eyes on her. She could hardly keep her eyes off of him. He looked even better in the daylight. Bianca couldn't remember the last time she'd seen someone so tall, dark and handsome. Last night in the bar, the dim light didn't do him justice. Before she realized it, she was undressing him with her eyes. She had to shake her head to get her mind out of the gutter.

Bianca tried to hurry up and finish with her current customer. The poor lady came in wanting a potion to give her cheating husband. She wanted to put the voodoo on the scoundrel as punition, punishment, for his cheating ways. Bianca chuckled to herself. Most of her business came from women who wanted to perform a ritual on their husband with a voodoo doll. Word must be getting around because they all came in with a lock of their husband's hair.

For a voodoo doll to be effective, that person had to really believe in what they were doing. Only if the person truly believed in the voodoo doll, then and only then would their wish be fulfilled.

Once the customer left, she moved towards him. She didn't realize how tall he was, she was almost a foot shorter than him. The closer Bianca moved to him, the more she felt the heat rising in her body.

She was attracted to this man, any woman would be attracted to him. He had a well defined body, one that she could spend hours exploring. He wore a t-shirt today that showed every ripple on his arms and chest. His blue jeans molded his body. She couldn't take her eyes off of his arms. He had the kind of arms you dreamed of having wrapped around you. She fantasized about what it would feel like to have those hands touch her; have his body joined with hers. He was pure male perfection and total eye candy. He would make any woman hungry just by looking at him.

When he finally spoke, she thought she would melt. The deepness of his accent was damned sexy. "I couldn't stop thinking about you last night and had to come check out your shop."

She looked at him dumbfounded, unsure of what to say for a moment, "I'm glad you decided to stop by. Would you like a tour?"

He smiled down at her and it was more than she could stand. She took in a deep breath to steady her nerves and inhaled his cologne. It was incredibly sexy and made her unstable on her feet. She looked up to find him watching her intently. Time seemed to stand still, their gazes locked.

This was the one man she should avoid falling for. Her grand-mere would warn her to stay clear of this man. That he had the devil in him.

Bianca couldn't fight the attraction she had for him though. He made her heart race. He was the best looking devil she had ever seen. Goosebumps crawled up her skin as he continued to look over her body.

Chapter 11

As Bianca Honore walked through the old streets, she made it to the cobblestone paved streets of the French Quarter. She was glad to be back home. There was no place else in the world like New Orleans. The people here were a mixture of cultures from the French, Spanish, Indian and African American legacies. Even some Italians had settled here in the late 1800s. Those who settled here included pirates, prisoners, pilgrims, adventurers, royalty and slaves just to name a few. The past was scarcely obscured here; the residents cherished their heritage and upbringing.

She had missed these sultry Louisiana nights, how the cool fog hung low against the levee at sunrise. She missed the sounds of the city, from the jazz that played at all hours to the sounds that rolled in from the river. She loved to breathe in the night air, hoping to catch a hint of the jasmine and magnolias that grew around the city. During the day she could smell the enticing scents of chicory coffee, red beans and rice, gumbo and boiled seafood.

Like many of the houses and shops in the French Quarter, the one that housed her voodoo shop was a narrow two story tall building. What appeared to be the front of the building that opened to the street was actually the back. The front of the building faced a quiet courtyard where her grand-mere grew some of her most prized herbs that she needed in a steady supply for the shop. There were also lush ferns and a fairly large water fountain nestled in the center of the beautiful courtyard. Unlike the cherubs or lions that adorned most of the fountains in this area, her grand-mere chose one that had a whimsical quality. It was a gargoyle that had water bubbling out from its mouth into the basin. There was also a wrought iron table and chairs nestled in one corner and a fire pit circled by stones that blackened over time when she performed certain voodoo rites.

As she unlocked the doors to the little shop, she took in her surroundings. There were several voodoo shops in the Quarter, but her grand-mere's shop was one of the more traditional ones. There was an apartment above the store as well, but her grand-mere preferred living in seclusion. Bianca moved into the apartment upstairs to be closer to work and the nightlife that New Orleans had to offer. She wondered why she had left here, there was something magical about this place.

While other cities attempted to capture the essence of New Orleans, none were successful. New Orleans had an ambiance all to itself. This city had a pulse, a rhythm, a life uniquely its own. The energy that thrived here could not be recreated. If she stood still, she could actually feel the pulse of the city.

Even the French Quarter had its own magic. Something about this place was surreal. There was an unmistakable feeling that lived here.

When she was younger, while her grand-mere was busy working in the shop, she would take one of the tours offered here. She loved to explore this city and discover all of its secrets.

A chill of exhilaration washed over Bianca as she watched the customer walk through the door. She couldn't wait for the day when they realized she was one of the most powerful voodoo priestesses since Marie Laveau. She'd heard rumors that there was another trying the same practices as her. Bianca was determined to find out who it was and inform this imposter that she would be the reigning Queen of Voodoo in New Orleans and no one else.

After Bianca had opened the shop, she took inventory of which ingredients and potions she needed to restock. She was low on the jars of powdered bone, spider legs and poison frog skin. She was also low on snake venom. It looked as if she would need to take a nightly jaunt down to the swamplands to obtain some more items for the store. Her grand-mere insisted on them foraging for ingredients to keep everything authentic for those who practiced voodoo. Bianca warned her customers that voodoo was not for amateurs and all the items in the store were authentic, which could be why they were so popular.

Bianca knew for a fact that several of the competitor's stores sold crushed bones as well, but upon closer scrutiny, it was merely crushed limestone. Her competitor's voodoo dolls were clearly factory stamped fabric dolls and cartoonish, whereas the dolls here were authentic versions. Some were even quite grotesque. They were made of black cloth or wax depending on the need of the doll, wrapped in scraps of fabric and had real human hair. For those that requested a voodoo doll to curse a certain individual, it had become known that if the customer brought in a lock of that person's hair, Bianca would incorporate it into the doll. This allowed them to control the person they wished to curse.

To keep the feel of the shop, Bianca had incense and cloves burning along with an audio CD of voodoo drums playing in the background. As she completed her inventory of the voodoo dolls, the door chime rang. Her newest customer must be a tourist and was uncomfortable being in the store. Bianca walked up to the woman and tried to put her at ease, "May I help you with something in particular?"

She let out a soft sigh, "A friend of mine suggested I visit one of these shops while I am down here. My husband passed away last year, and I am worried he is still on this earth instead of at peace."

She looked at the woman and smiled while thinking to herself that this would be easy money. "Why don't we see if we can summon up your husband's spirit and ask him?"

She saw the woman hesitate, "Do you really think you can do that?"

"I can try."

"How much do you charge?"

She placed the lady's hands in hers, "I won't charge you until we are done. I want to make sure that you are satisfied. If so, then we can talk price. Before we begin, I must ask the name of your husband."

"George. George Holden."

Bianca held out the chair for her newest customer and sat across from her. She chanted and slowly rocked back and forth, shaking a small brass rattle. Inside the rattle were small snake vertebrae bones. Her chanting turned to low mumbling and then she made herself clear once again. "Oh spirits, we humbly ask that you send the spirit of this woman's beloved husband, George Holden, to join us."

Time seemed to stand still for a moment before the candles in the room flickered. Bianca informed Mrs. Holden, "George is here with us."

Mrs. Holden watched as the candles in the room continued to flicker and shadows danced on the wall. A cold draft swept across the room. Suddenly, the smell of her late husband's cologne filled the room, bringing tears to her eyes.

Mrs. Holden asked out, "George? George is that really you?"

"George wants to let you know that he has moved on, and that he loves you very much."

Her eyes stayed glued to Bianca, "Tell him that I love him very much too, and I miss him dearly."

"He wants you to go and enjoy yourself on this cruise. You will make plenty of new friends."

She let out a surprised gasp. "George isn't upset with me for spending money on the cruise is he?"

She shook her head, "No. He wants you to go and don't let Gloria make you feel guilty about going."

She grasped Bianca's hands, "Oh my. Thank you so much for doing this."

Bianca smiled, "I am so glad you found the answers you were looking for."

She took a tissue from her purse and dabbed at the tears in her eyes, "Oh, yes I did. Thank you so much. I felt guilty about going on the cruise, but not anymore. George was right; I was letting Gloria Anderson make me feel guilty about going on this trip. I was ready to call it off, but not now."

"No, George and I both think this trip will do you a world of good. You will make plenty of new friends on this trip."

She watched as the customer reached into her wallet and pulled out two crisp one hundred dollar bills. "Here, this is for you. I hope it is enough."

Bianca smiled at the lady, "You are too kind. Thank you so much. When you get back, you must stop by and tell me all about it."

"Yes, I will do just that."

As the woman left her shop, two giggling college girls entered and she let out a groan. She doubted these two had any money and wanted a potion of some kind, more than likely a love potion.

"Can I help you ladies?"

"My friend here has a date, finally. I want to find her a charm that will help her get lucky."

Bianca shook her head, "Mais non, she doesn't need a charm for that. She needs to make him wait before sleeping with the young man."

The young girl scoffed at her, "What, like until the second date?"

Bianca looked at the other young girl and informed her, "You must make a man desire you. The longer you make him wait, the more his desire for you will be."

Her friend replied, "Yeah, right. He will just move on and find someone who will give him a piece of ass."

Bianca folded her arms and stared at the girl scornfully, "Mais, this man may be special to your friend." She turned and looked at the other young girl, "Do not rush into bed with this young man. Make him respect you first. He is obviously attracted to you or he wouldn't have asked you out. Let him get to know you before you rush into bed with him."

Bianca gently escorted the girl to the display she had set up of cowrie shells. She informed the young girl, "Don't pay your friend no mind. You see these shells here. They are called cowrie shells. They are used for prosperity and love spells."

The young girl picked up one and studied it intently. Bianca continued, "Each shell resembles a woman's sexual center. I can use one of these if you desire to put a love spell on your young man."

The girl looked at her in awe, "You seriously do spells?"

She looked directly into the girl's eyes, "Voodoo is not something to be played with. The spells I conjure up are quite effective. The only time the effect becomes neutralized is when the person who asked for the spell doesn't believe in voodoo."

The young girl set the shell back down, "I don't know about casting a spell."

Her friend let out a laugh, "She is pulling your leg. This stuff doesn't work. It is just for fun. Come on and find you a charm so we can go."

Bianca waved her hands at the troublesome friend, wishing she could cast a spell on the girl and be done with her. Except they were paying customers and she didn't want to lose a sale. "If you want I can give you a reading."

The girl asked, "What kind of reading?"

"I can give you a tarot card reading or if you want we can cast the shells."

"What do you mean cast the shells?"

"It is another way of fortune telling. It is a form of Obi Divination. You will cast the cowrie shells and the answer will come as the shells fall. Would you like a reading?"

She agreed, "It might be fun. Let's give it a try."

The young girls followed Bianca back to the small room she used for readings. Inside the room were dozens of candles and a strong smell of incense burning.

They sat around the small table. Bianca asked, "Do you want to know about the boy you are seeing tonight?"

The girl shook her head, "No, let's do a general reading."

"As you wish." Bianca instructed her to shuffle the cards seven times. While waiting for her to shuffle the cards, she closed her eyes and rested her hands on the table, palms upward.

Once done, she instructed the young girl, "Cut the deck and hand me eleven cards, one at a time."

Bianca laid out the first three cards, left to right. She arranged the remaining cards at North, East, South and West around the group of three.

Bianca studied the cards, "A new romance is in your future, but it is not from whom you suspect. However," Bianca pointed to a card, "you must be careful of those you trust. Someone means to stop that romance." Bianca looked at the other friend fairly certain this girl meant nothing but harm to her friend's future.

The two girls giggled at the warning. Bianca pointed to another card, "This one is a seven of swords, and this card is the eight of staves. They talk of deception. You must be careful of those you trust with your secrets. But don't give up hope because the cards also tell of heart, love and prosperity, a true connection in your future."

After the last customer left for the day, Bianca felt restless and went for a walk. The evening sun felt good on her skin. The day had left her drained. She knew the two girls didn't take much stock in what she had to say, but she had to warn the timid girl that her friend was up to no good.

With everyone getting off of work, the streets were congested. The local cafes were busy preparing for the dinner service, rushing to make sure the outdoor tables were ready. Street vendors were moving their carts off the road now that the lunch time rush was over. Only a few of the street vendors remained open after dark.

As she walked down Bourbon Street, she breathed in the air. She loved the nighttime in New Orleans. It became more festive at night; the air even seemed to change. Instead of the aromatic smell of coffee filling the air, it was a blend of spices and seafood from the restaurants cooking for their dinner service.

As she walked down Rampart Street, she observed the damage left behind from Hurricane Katrina. Several buildings still showed the true impact the hurricane had on the city. She could look up and see the flood lines on the buildings. In this area, there remained quite a few abandoned shops. Her grand-mere had been lucky that her shop in the French Quarter did not suffer as much damage as other businesses.

***

That night as Bianca slept, her grand-mere came to visit her. She sat on the edge of the bed and looked at Bianca with sadness in her eyes. "Trouble is coming your way. You must be ready. I know you have it inside of yourself to banish this evil from your life."

Before Bianca could tell her not to worry, she faded away.

Chapter 12

Alexis Lemoine dreaded this day for quite some time. She'd tried to talk her parents out of the arranged marriage between her and Dominic St. Germaine for the last six months, but they refused to listen. They kept telling her it was a tradition that would be upheld. They didn't want to upset the St. Germaine Family after what they had been through recently. Besides, the marriage was arranged at their birth.

Alexis had hoped with the death of Saul St. Germaine, Dominic would see reason and inform her parents that the arranged marriage need not take place. He, however, was just as set on traditions as her parents. He told her that they would marry and at the end of the year he would freely give her a divorce.

At least the next year wouldn't be as bad as she first feared. Dominic St. Germaine was a handsome man and maybe her mother was correct, and she would come to love Dominic as much as her mother loved her father.

She must admit that Dominic had been loving and respectful while courting her as their parents planned the wedding. Since the death of Mr. St. Germaine, the original wedding date would be postponed to allow Dominic time to adjust and the Family time to grieve. That was fine with Alexis; the additional time gave her a chance to get to know Dominic better.

The wedding ceremony would take place at the cathedral with the reception taking place at the St. Germaine plantation. From there they planned to honeymoon in Bora

Bora before coming back to the plantation to live in wedded bliss, if there was such a thing.

***

Dominic should be wooing his future bride, but he could not get his mind off of the girl he saw the other day. He noticed her walking down Bourbon Street and followed her into the little shop. He also saw her in a bar one night, but she was talking to Alfonso Scarcelli. A few nights later, he and his friends met up with her in that same bar. He would love to steal a girl away from that man. Bianca Honore was not only an attractive woman, but also exactly the person he needed to put his plan into motion. He would avenge his father's death, and he suspected that she could help him. When talking to her, he could tell that they were kindred spirits. He did a little digging on Bianca Honore. From what he ascertained, she liked to hang out with some questionable characters in New York when living there, people known to practice voodoo, especially black magic. He could barely contain the exhilaration of all they could do together.

Chapter 13

Teresa and Alfonso decided to go out to eat and celebrate their union. This last month of wedded bliss had been exceptionally pleasant, and they seemed to be adjusting well to their new way of life. Most nights he came home late and slept in one of the guest rooms as to not wake her.

In return for her not questioning where he had been or asking if he had a mistress, he allowed her to go shopping wherever she pleased. She had been to New York, Los Angeles, and San Francisco already and spent tens of thousands of dollars. She had the closet that she'd always dreamed of and more shoes than she would ever be able to wear. Still, that didn't stop her from shopping and spending her husband's money.

For dinner tonight he took her out to one of the more elegant restaurants here. She wanted him to fly her to Paris, but he was too busy to leave the state, much less the country. He spent most of his time talking to his second in command about the new Families moving in. She wasn't worried and had complete faith in his capabilities. She had witnessed his temper, though, and would hate to be one of his enemies. The other night during a meeting, she stepped into the kitchen and one of his bodyguards looked at her with lustful eyes. Alfonso took out his gun and pistol whipped him in an instant. The young man hadn't been seen since and no one dared to speak his name. Alfonso may not love her, but he had a jealous streak when it came to someone wanting what he owned. If he became that jealous over someone or something that he didn't care about, she could just imagine what he would do if someone tried to take something he did love.

By the time they returned home, it was storming outside. They were drenched when they made it inside. Alfonso went to light a fire in the fireplace and she walked into the study to pour them a drink. She poured a Maker's Mark on the rocks for him and a glass of Chardonnay for her. When she walked into the living room, the sight of her husband took her breath away. There was something incredibly sexy about a man stoking a fire. She walked over to him and handed him his drink.

She heard the fire crackling in the fireplace and the rain hitting the window outside. Lightning streaked across the night sky and thunder shook the old house. She jumped at the sudden noise. When he pulled her into his arms, it was her undoing. She saw the hunger in his eyes when he looked down at her.

His hand slid up her rib cage in a tantalizing touch that was only his. He whispered in her ear, "You already want me don't you?"

She smirked at him, "And why do you think that?"

"I can feel you tremble in my arms."

She let out a soft laugh, "You are mighty full of yourself tonight aren't you?"

In one fluid movement, he lifted her up and carried her off to the bedroom. The rain continued to pelt against the French doors in the bedroom as thunder rumbled through the house, and the lightning outside created a soft glow in the room; the weather outside matched her mood, tempestuous. She reached up and stroked his hard jaw. The feeling of her hand on his face broke all the restraint he had. He brought his mouth to her neck and sent electric kisses down her body. His free hand made short work of slipping her out of her dress.

She reveled in the fact that he was the most skilled and masterful lover she had ever had. He knew all the right places to touch her and always had her begging for more. She allowed him to have full control of her body.

He rubbed the length of his body up and over her while gently nipping at her body. She felt completely helpless to his will as desire rushed through her body. He loved having her under his control, having her surrender to him. His very touch made her want him. She could only imagine how many lovers it took to develop this amount of expertise.

She felt his hot breath along her already heated skin. She let out a soft moan as he kissed her once more. Her skin sizzled from his lips.

He gave her a wicked smile, "I love to touch you. Your skin is so soft." His hands continued to torment her body as they ran up and down her legs. She could see the passion he felt for her in his eyes.

Chapter 14

As the Mafia Prince listened to the morning reports from his workers, he kept looking at his watch. He wanted to be at Bianca's shop as soon as it opened. Not only did he want to see her again, but he wanted to get to know her a little better. Before he could approach her with what he had to propose, he needed to be one hundred percent positive that their business relationship would work. If she were too meek and mild to do what he had in mind, then he would keep looking. Maybe someone she had worked with in New York would be interested in assisting him with his plans. There was also the possibility that someone in Haiti would be willing as well. He didn't want someone that dabbled in black magic; he wanted someone who would take this all the way. If he played his cards right, he could become one of the most powerful families in the United States and would never again have to get near his enemies and opponents.

When it was his turn to talk, everyone listened intently, "Thank y'all for catching me up. I need to inform you of a few things as well. The Devereauxs are not playing by the rules we have set since my father's death. Some of their guys have been seen talking to our girls. We need to let them know that is not how we do business here. They have to realize the St. Germaine Family is the top dog around this town."

Brian asked, "What the hell is their problem?"

The Mafia Prince didn't like the fact that the Devereauxs were getting this ballsy. The Devereaux family needed to be stopped before they tried to get any bigger. They started off with loan sharking and then they made friends with some drug cartel members. From there, they grew. They weren't as smart as his Family, though. No, his Family knew to keep a low profile; you needed a legitimate business to hide behind. Their Family and their name were respected; it emitted power here; whereas the Devereaux Family name meant nothing to most in this town.

He responded, "I am not sure. They are starting to get in the way. The other day I received several reports that their men are trying to collect from my businesses as well."

The Mafia Prince didn't divulge too much information. He suspected he had a snitch and he planned to give each of them different information to weed out those that couldn't be trusted. When he learned the identity of the snitch, that person would wish they had never been born. When you worked for a Mafia Family, loyalty was something you didn't mess with.

His men were anxious to show the Devereaux Family who the top dog was. They would get their chance soon enough, but first, he planned on talking to Bianca to see how she could help him. He knew for certain that she was not the snitch, but he had to make sure she could be trusted.

Between the voodoo dolls and potions, he would be unstoppable. He would be the biggest Mafia Family here in the United States and Italy once he combined forces as he planned. Right now, his Family consisted of seventy members, but he hoped to increase those numbers as soon as possible. He also had over five hundred associates, but once he became international, he would be the King of the Mafia not just the Mafia Prince.

From everything he'd learned about Bianca and her family, she had the knowledge and the right background for what he'd planned. Her deceased grand-mere was a well-known voodoo priestess. She had been well respected in the parish, hell the state, for her knowledge. She was born a traiteur or healer. However, from everything the Mafia Prince learned about the old woman, she was very much against the black magic. Could this be one of the reasons Bianca moved to New York, to learn the black magic her grand-mere refused to teach her? The only problem was that he could not bring something like this up in simple conversation, especially if she felt the same way as her grand-mere about the subject.

When it was time to leave, he had a spring in his step. He couldn't wait to see what the day brought. Ever since he'd met Bianca in the bar that night, he could not get her image out of his mind. This could be a mistake, especially with a new wife, but a mistake he was willing to make, especially if this worked out as he planned.

As he entered the store, the scent of incense invaded his nostrils. As soon as she saw him enter the shop, she smiled up at him, "What brings you back so soon? Did you finally decide on a reading?"

He replied with a wicked smile, placing his hand on his chest, "I think you put a voodoo hex on me. I can't get you out of my mind."

She let out a soft laugh that sent hot desire rushing through his veins. "Would you like to stop by the hotel tonight and have supper with me? We can eat in the penthouse where we will have complete privacy or we can eat in the dining room so that I can show off a beautiful woman."

She gave him a sultry smile, "I can swing an early supper in the penthouse. I've never seen that floor. It is a beautiful hotel and I have always wondered what the penthouse looked like."

"We will have to make sure you get your wish then. I will instruct the chef to prepare us something extra special. Do you have a favorite?"

"I have a very healthy appetite. Surprise me."

***

Bianca couldn't wait for the day to end. She had something to do tonight and the day drug on. By the time she made it to the hotel, she was a bundle of nerves. She had never felt this way for a man before and chided herself in the way she was behaving. He was a man and she was a woman; therefore, it was only natural to feel some desire for the attractive man. But there was more to it than that, fate brought them together.

As she took the elevator to the penthouse floor, she felt the butterflies in her stomach. If she'd had any doubts about the Mafia rumors, they were quickly answered when she entered the elevator to the penthouse. It was a good thing he'd informed his staff of her impending arrival. If not, she probably would have been strip searched before being thrown out on her ear. She wondered where he found his body guards. She had never seen so many muscles on anyone. She swore that even his ears had muscles. Where on earth did he find his clothes?

Bianca's nerves were stretched so thin she could barely taste the exquisite meal. After supper, he refilled their wine glasses and they stepped out onto the balcony. She watched as he pulled out a cigar and puffed on it. They stood there for a while looking at the New Orleans scenery without speaking. Even without talking or touching, she sensed his presence.

He suddenly turned to her, with his chest against her while he looked down at her. Desire coiled through her body, warming her blood. She felt the heat emanating from his body.

Time seemed to stand still as they continued to look at one another, as if daring the other person to make the next move. Bianca felt his hands on her waist and she stepped in closer to him. His lips touched hers faintly. His warm breath mixed with her own ragged breath. She deepened the kiss as he pulled her closer to him.

She had no control over her body. Even if she wanted to tell him no, she couldn't. The passion for him became all consuming. All she could do was feel! The sensations coming from his fingertips were pure torture.

He moved back to her lips, nibbling at her lower lip before once again devouring her mouth with his. Slowly, expertly, he slid his tongue over her lips and delved into her mouth.

Bianca closed her eyes and felt his hands on her back. His other hand pulled her even closer until their bodies were almost one. It still wasn't close enough for her. She wanted to be one with him. She wanted him to consume her.

***

He had no idea what came over him. He'd planned to get to know her better during this visit. He shouldn't be this close to her; if they became business associates, sex would get in the way. His father stressed the importance of never mixing business with pleasure and those were words he lived by. However, being this close to her drove him mad.

He couldn't take being this close to her any longer. He
wondered if she had any idea of the power she had over
him. He searched her eyes to see if she wanted this as well.
When he found his answer, he brought his lips down to her
neck and kissed the line of her jaw.

Chapter 15

When he first approached Bianca about his plan to become one of the strongest Families in New Orleans, she warned him that there was a price to pay when dealing with the spirits. Before she started her ceremony a warm gust of wind blew through the room. The candle flames flickered but did not extinguish. Even the lights dimmed dramatically and long shadows danced along the wall. For a moment, Bianca's heart stopped. Surely, this couldn't be a warning from the spirits. She quickly made a sign of the cross as the warmth that suffocated her in this room turned cold.

Bianca took in this large room where she would start her new venture. She was given an open budget and permitted to purchase whatever she wanted for her black magic. Bianca had made several trips recently to the Amazon. Scattered throughout were various plants of every conceivable shape and form. There were also vials of essential oils, fish poisons, mahogany carvings, and dozens of hand blown glass jars with various concoctions. She had an altar set up as well as a special altar for all of her voodoo dolls. With these dolls, she could cause pain to any of her Boss's enemies without ever venturing close to them.

One vial contained her most precious toxin, a powder that when absorbed into the skin would make the victim appear dead, but they were very much alive. The drug lowered the metabolic state of the victim. They would essentially become the walking dead. Excitement pulsed through her body at just the thought of using this drug on a victim. She had the antidote, but she never intended to use it on her victims.

She walked over to the man restrained in the chair in the middle of the room. She told her Boss she could get this man to talk, and she meant to prove it. She had great plans for this one; he would be the first to try her new potion. She was anxious to see if it worked the way it should and now was her chance.

***

Brad Sullivan woke up to find himself restrained to a chair. He tried to make himself more comfortable when he realized he wasn't alone. He peered into the dark room to see who else was there. The candlelight barely gave any illumination to the room. If the bastard thought he could scare him into talking, he had another thing coming to him. He had been trained to take pain and not break a sweat. In his line of business, it was important to take as much pain as you could dish out. He had been taught that there would be those who would torture him to get him to talk and for that very reason he inflicted pain on himself to numb his body to the sensations. Let them try their worst; it would not work on him.

He waited for the goon squad to come in at any minute and break fingers, then bones. He shook his head. He still couldn't believe they'd finally captured him. He should have known not to let his guard down, even for a beautiful woman.

***

This one would be difficult; she could see it in his eyes. He was angry, not afraid. The Mafia Prince looked over at her and nodded his head. She began to work her magic. He had stressed the importance of how he needed the man to talk and answer certain questions before the prisoner was hers. Even after using some of her stronger potions, his will remained strong and he gave vague answers. She increased the amount of her special potion to encourage him to talk more freely. It had to be done slowly or his body would go into shock; she had her own reasons for not wanting this one dead. Her Boss may want answers, but she wanted to experiment with this one. She wanted to know if the zombie potion worked on a man as strong willed as this one. He had yet to be intimidated.

This was the best high she had ever had. She couldn't wait to continue this journey.

Afterwards, the Mafia Prince walked over to her, "Are you okay with what happened tonight?"

"Cher, do not feel guilty. I wanted to do this."

He replied, "Yeah, but you didn't grow up in this world like I did. It can take some getting used to, with me, it is in my blood. My father always said that I had a gift and was born for this very job. There are others in this field that are proficient, but they aren't born with the intuition that one needs for this job. Some have dreams and can't get what they do out of their minds, those are the ones that will turn on you."

"You have given me the opportunity I was looking for. I get to practice my black magic." She brought his head down to hers and kissed him on the mouth. "Thank you for giving me my dream cher."

***

At first he had been surprised at how well she had taken his unusual request. Even his father scoffed at the idea, but not this woman. She was enthusiastic about it. If the others had an opinion about him working with a voodoo priestess, they didn't voice their opinions. They knew to treat him with respect and to always carry out his orders.

As much as he missed his father, he knew he was doing the right thing. His dad had prepared the businessmen that his son would take over for him soon. His dad had other ventures he wanted to oversee himself and would leave the main part of the business under his command. Even though he still went by the Mafia Prince, everyone knew that he was the one in charge. Besides, when they called him the Mafia Prince, it was a term of endearment and a nickname he'd had since birth.

He knew when he met Bianca that everything in his life happened for a reason. Something told him to go to that bar that night. They were drawn to each other like moths to a flame. She completed him; he could be his true self in front of her.

Chapter 16

Bianca watched the newly married couple dance from her hiding spot. She would love to put a voodoo curse on the new Mrs. Dominic St. Germaine, but that would bring HIS wrath down heavy on Bianca and she did not want that. She had fallen hard for Dominic and he swore that she was the one he wanted, but this marriage had been arranged long before they met. He promised his new wife that they only had to be married for a short year, and then he would let her go. This would be the longest year of Bianca's life, but at least, she had her work.

As Bianca watched the happy couple dance at their wedding reception, her hatred for the new bride was once again ignited. She clearly remembered the day she first met Alexis Lemoine; Bianca was six years old and Alexis was nine.

Bianca's mother worked for the Lemoine family as a cook at that time. She went in the mornings to cook their breakfast and came home after the dinner dishes were cleared away. Growing up, Bianca ate breakfast early if she wanted it hot. Bianca's supper was always late when her mom had to cook. Most days, her grand-mere cooked supper.

On that fateful day when Bianca met Alexis Lemoine for the first time, Bianca begged her mom to go to work with her. There was no school that week because of Mardi Gras and Bianca didn't want to spend the day at her grand-mere's shop; she wanted to spend time with her mother. After promising her mother that she would not get into any trouble, her mother allowed her to go with her.

It so happened that day Alexis was celebrating her birthday and her mother was preparing everything for the party.

Bianca watched as her mother busily prepared the elegant dining room for the birthday cake. Bianca had never seen so much pink. Someone had already put up pink balloons and streamers throughout the room. To this day, Bianca couldn't stand the color pink.

They had fancy pink plates and glasses for the guests to use. Over the years, Bianca had come to learn that the plates and glasses were made of Depression glass. She'd never seen anything like it before. She was in total awe at the sight of the dining room. Her whole house could probably fit in that one big room.

While Bianca's mother was finalizing everything in the room for the party, she instructed Bianca to start washing dishes. This was one chore that Bianca enjoyed. It was the one time her mother allowed her to play in the warm sudsy water as much as she wanted, just as long as the dishes were cleaned in the process. She piled soap bubbles as high as she could before blowing them away. The more she played in the water the more bubbles there were. Her mother figured this would keep her from getting underfoot.

Bianca was having so much fun when Alexis entered the kitchen; she didn't even notice her. She must have been quite a sight now that she thought about it, but at that time all she could think about was how mean the girl had been.

Bianca was playing in the water and her clothes were soaking wet. Her mother had been cooking in the kitchen and Bianca's unruly hair had started to frizz because of the heat.

When Alexis walked into the kitchen, she gawked at Bianca before bursting into giggles. Bianca had never seen a girl as pretty as her. She had the greenest eyes with black hair. The two things together created quite a contrast. She even had a green dress and a hair bow that matched the color of her eyes giving them a depth Bianca envied. Bianca's hazel eyes only showed a vivid green when she was upset. Bianca felt dowdy next to this girl. She even had on shiny black leather shoes that probably cost more than her mother could ever afford.

She wished she had such striking looks. When Alexis laughed at Bianca, she knew this girl certainly was not as pretty on the inside as she was on the outside. To make it worse, the mean girl brought her friends into the kitchen so they could get a good laugh.

Bianca had been so embarrassed. As she raised a finger to put a curse on the awful girls, her mother walked into the room. She pushed Bianca's finger down before she could do any harm and ushered the other girls into the dining room.

While the girls were busy with the birthday party and her mother was tending to their every need, Bianca slipped out of the house and went in search of something to scare the mean girl. As she made her way to the river, she found what she was looking for - a little grass snake.

Bianca learned at an early age how to handle even the most poisonous of snakes. Her grand-mere collected cottonmouths to defang. They were important in some of the voodoo rituals. The snake was thought to give you supernatural powers when performing your voodoo practice. She also collected the venom from the cottonmouths and rattle snakes to use in potions.

Bianca carefully captured the snake and hid it in her shirt. She held back the giggles as it slithered about. She peeked into the dining room and noticed the pile of gifts on the buffet. She immediately knew what to do.

Bianca snuck into the room and hid behind the heavy velvet damask drapes that flanked the French doors. She found a gift box she could easily slip the snake into. Before leaving her hiding spot, she made sure no one saw her.

As Bianca finished up the dishes, a scream tore through the house. She let out a soft giggle. It served the little princess right. And to make it even better, Alexis was so scared that she peed in her panties in front of all of her friends and her friends laughed at her. Bianca had been scared that she would be found out, but instead, Alexis's little brother was reprimanded since he was always taunting his older sister with snakes. Bianca didn't feel bad that he got in trouble for her prank either; he was just as mean as his sister. He called Bianca names behind her mother's back.

Later that night, Bianca's mother reprimanded her for trying to put a voodoo curse on those girls, explaining that if she ever did that then Bianca's mother would never find work again.

As Bianca watched the couple enjoy their day, jealousy rushed through her body. She couldn't wait a year before Dominic made her his. She had to get rid of this woman. She wondered if Alexis even remembered that they'd met when they were children. Alexis was one of her faithful customers at the shop and had never mentioned anything. She came in at least once a week to have her palm or tarot cards read. She even came to have a reading right before the wedding.

Dominic swore he didn't love his new wife, but Bianca saw the way he looked at her and she had seen the cards. She needed to break up this marriage before they realized that they loved each other.

As Bianca watched the happy couple, she despised the fact that they made the perfect couple on the outside. Would Alexis think of Dominic in the same way if she knew all of his secrets? Mais non, Bianca couldn't see this prim and proper girl going for any of the things that Dominic enjoyed.

Unable to take watching the festivities anymore, she headed over to where she had her ginseng planted. She needed more ginseng root for the shop. Her grand-mere taught her that the root would cure the part of the body that it resembled the most. When a customer asked for a remedy for an ailment for a specific body part, she ground up the root that best fit the circumstance for their use.

Chapter 17

The Mafia Prince walked around the newly renovated hotel and casino with pride. This was turning out to be a profitable venture and a wise decision.

It was named on The New Orleans Most Extravagant Hotels and Casinos list. All of the high rollers came here to play and stay. They demanded the best, and he ensured his staff met their needs. It was the only stop for the rich and pampered.

The place was busy tonight; there wasn't a spare seat available at the blackjack tables. As he made his way to the cocktail lounge, he saw Teresa walk into the lobby. She gracefully moved through the lobby and slid into a back booth in the lounge. She didn't notice him watching her and he ducked into the shadows to see what she was doing. Since he could not get a good look at her from where he was standing, he headed over to the security office. He instructed the guard sitting behind the security desk to zoom the camera in on her. As he studied her beautiful face, he noticed her mesmerizing eyes. He'd never realized how green they actually were. Her lush auburn hair fell in luxurious waves down her back. This woman was not only gorgeous, but she had a resilient nature about her as well as class.

Just as she always did, she wore clothes and jewelry that the average woman could never afford. He wondered if she knew she attracted attention wherever she went. Her very demeanor screamed a woman of great wealth and privilege. He had a feeling other women felt inferior in her presence.

A sinister smile formed across his face as he watched the man sit opposite from her at the table. She must be having a little rendezvous. This may be just the leverage he needed.

He looked down at the security guard, "I want her every move recorded while she is here. Do not take the cameras or your eyes off of her do you understand?"

"Yes, sir."

"Good, as soon as she leaves come up to my office with the DVD."

"Yes, sir."

***

Teresa walked into the hotel lobby and made her way to the lounge. She was unsure of whether she should be meeting this man here or not, but her father asked her to do this for him and she would do anything for him. Her loyalties lay with him and not her husband.

Her dad feared that the Scarcelli Family was hiding the success of the American businesses from him and he wanted someone he trusted to infiltrate the business here to find out. Her cousin Antonio flew down from Italy to help him. They were meeting here so that she could discuss everything with him before he met with Alfonso.

She saw Antonio walk into the lounge and waved him over, "Ciao Antonio. How was your flight?"

"It was good. Does Alfonso know that your dad sent me over?"

"No, he does not. We don't want Alfonso to know that we are related. If he knew that you were my blood kin, he might not trust you. No, you need to start at the bottom and gain his trust. I know he is looking for a new henchman and tomorrow morning you will meet with him. Joey will introduce you."

"And who is this Joey?"

"Joey is one of his snitches on the street. You don't have to worry about Joey. I promised Joey some primo heroin if he introduced you as a half-assed wiseguy."

"Okay then. What else do I need to know?"

Before she could answer him the waitress arrived, "Can I get y'all something to drink?"

She looked at the waitress, "I will have a Limoncello."

"And for you, sir?"

"I will have a Martini, please."

He looked over at his cousin, "I still haven't gotten used to these American drinks."

"The bars around here cater to us Italians just as they do to their own. I think it is because there are so many Italians here."

"That may be, but the alcohol isn't near as good as in Italy."

She laughed at him, "You are just spoiled. You will get used to it here. There are a lot of Italian shops around here. You won't miss home too much; I promise."

"We shall see. I am glad that your dad asked me to help him out, though."

She looked him directly in the eyes, "You do understand that this can be dangerous, don't you?"

He shrugged his shoulders, "I would do anything for your pops. He has always been good to me."

She took out a cigarette and lit it. As she leaned back in her seat, she took a long drag on the cigarette before blowing the smoke out of her mouth. "These men can be dangerous. Some are no better than animals, vicious and bloodthirsty. They have no feelings whatsoever. They have their own ambitions and most want to be Alfonso's right hand man now that his dad is gone. You must be one of them now. Learn how to fit in."

"You worry too much. You forget; I grew up in this lifestyle. I know how to take care of myself. Taking a risk doesn't scare me."

She shook her head, "No, but these men don't have the same respect for the Family as they do back home. Here, all they think about are the rewards that come with this lifestyle."

They stopped talking as the waitress approached with their drinks. After she placed their drinks on the table, she asked, "Will there be anything else?"

Antonio replied, "I'll call you back if we do need anything." With a wave of his hand, he dismissed her.

She informed him, "I have lived this life as well, but these men are not the same as the ones we grew up with. They are not taught the same respect."

Chapter 18

He breathed in the night air. It was springtime and the river carried with it the smell of replenished life. Already, the trees were showing signs of life once again. The pear and redbud trees were in full bloom; their heady fragrance filled the night air. In the distance, he heard an alligator as it made a splash into the water. It was more than likely looking for something to eat or possibly building itself a new nest out of the sticks, sand and river mud that lined the area.

Fog rolled in off of the Mississippi River, somehow obscuring the full moon completely. All that remained was the midnight glow of moisture that permeated the clouds and now flowed effortlessly across the ground. From where he stood, it looked as if skeletal fingers were reaching out to him. He involuntarily stepped back. Without warning, the air temperature dropped and the night life became silent.

The Mafia Prince looked around to make sure no one was lurking about. The wind whipped through the trees, and the branches blew restlessly in the breeze. Even the night seemed to be preparing itself. The moon peeked through the fog and stared down on the plantation as if it was curious.

It was the perfect place to allow Bianca to perform her outside rituals. No one would come near here. This land had belonged to his family for centuries. Once, slaves toiled this land to grow cotton or whatever other crops his family decided to grow. The produce was loaded onto barges that sailed up and down the river and brought right into the port of New Orleans to be sold.

The plantation house was inspired by Greek architecture, with towering columns and more rooms than would ever be used. The house boasted plenty of ornate furniture bought by family members over the years as well as delicate china, crystal chandeliers, antiques and gilt edged wainscoting. An antique dealer would have an orgasm as soon as they entered the home.

As the family's wealth increased, so did the items in the house. His mom spent money as fast as his dad made it. His dad had a knack for investing money and over the years he'd bought stock in several profitable companies.

His Family ruled this parish with an iron fist over the last century, not only in politics but in employment and sheer brutality. His Family had not always been a wealthy, influential Family, but strove to become one the strongest criminal Families here.

His ancestors were not known to be kind and were feared by many. He planned to change the way things were run. He wanted his enemies to never know he was coming, to hide his crimes from the authorities.

The sound of the drums accompanied by the horns suddenly filled the night air. The eerie sound even had his men on edge.

He watched in awe as Bianca moved up to the shrine. No matter how many times she performed this ritual, her movements kept him mesmerized. Soon, she would make those who crossed him pay. She took each of the tiny dolls in her hands and began her curse.

Chapter 19

Bianca carefully prepared the potion for James Fontaine's wife. She would be at the shop later this afternoon for a reading. While Amanda Fontaine was here, Bianca would tell her that she saw something wicked lurking between her and her husband. Bianca planned to have Amanda believe her husband was having an affair. Bianca would then give her a potion to give him, but she would warn her only to use a small amount of this potion. All she needed to do was to rub a small portion onto his skin.

Bianca would leave out the fact not get it on her skin. Amanda was an attractive woman and would make an excellent addition to their growing collection of women. They would soon have another auction to sell off some more women. With the women as zombies, they were easier to control. Those that were too strong for the potion to work on, they had ways of dealing with as well.

Bianca picked up a jar of crushed bone and inspected it. With a devilish smile on her face, she wondered whose bones were in this jar. Her grand-mere would be greatly disappointed in her for practicing black magic, but with each spell she cast, her power grew stronger. She had yet to find out who else in this town was practicing the black magic, but she would not give up until she did. Bianca was slowly bringing followers down from New York to join her, being careful who she invited since she wanted to be the voodoo priestess here and not share control.

When the Mafia Prince came up with the idea to eliminate his enemies without them knowing, Bianca had been a little jealous that she did not think of it first. It was brilliant.

Bianca prepared a special potion for him, and now he never needed to get close to them.

***

The need to see Bianca overcame the Mafia Prince. Instead of going home to his wife, he went to visit his voodoo priestess. That woman had a hold on him. He loved his wife dearly, but Bianca was the only one that satisfied his primal needs. His wife would balk at the things Bianca did for him, as would his other mistresses. He found it difficult to stay faithful no matter how hard he tried.

As he neared Bianca's small cabin, he smelled food cooking. His mouth watered at the tantalizing smells that assailed his senses as he approached the cabin. His stomach let out a growl, reminding him that he hadn't eaten since that morning.

He walked in the door and smiled at the sight of Bianca busy at the stove, singing a little tune and dancing in place. "It smells fantastic in here." He peered into the pot to see what she was cooking. Teasingly, he asked, "That's not a potion is it?"

She swatted at his hand, "Mais, as if. You know very well this is my gumbo pot."

He loved agitating her. She had a spirit in her that he loved to rile. He asked, "Did you put okra in it?"

"Now what kind of question is that? You know damn well that I always put okra in my gumbo. I even went out this morning and picked it fresh from the garden."

He smiled at her as he wrapped his arms tightly around her waist to bring her closer to him. This was another area where Bianca and his wife differed. His new bride thought food should come from the store, or a restaurant when possible. Bianca believed in growing as much of her food as possible. It all came down to their upbringing.   His wife came from a wealthy family that dined out as much as possible. Whereas Bianca's family were hard working common people who believed in living off of the land.

Where his wife couldn't even boil water, Bianca could cook up a plate of food in no time flat.

Deciding to ruffle Bianca's feathers a little more, he teased, "You didn't let your roux darken enough. It's too light!"

She turned in his arms and glared at him, "Mais you know better. I have told you that a dark roux is bad for your stomach. It is the perfect honey color and easier on your stomach."

He kissed her on the nose. "It is so easy to get you going, you know that?"

***

When his stomach let out another loud growl, she pushed him toward the small table in the kitchen, "Go sit. I will fix us a bite to eat."

She enjoyed feeding this man. Her momma always said the way to a man's heart was through his stomach, and this one had mentioned more than once that his new wife didn't cook. Two things that kept him coming back to her were cooking and performing all the various acts that he enjoyed so well.

She remembered her momma telling her that for her fairy tales to come true, she had to make it happen. With each passing day, she came even closer to achieving what she wanted. There had been trials and tribulations along the way, but it would be well worth what it if she ended up with her true love.

Chapter 20

Dominic gave Bianca permission to walk around the property in search of herbs and other items for her shop. She was busy searching for everything she needed when she noticed a car coming up the long driveway. Curious, she headed towards the house and moved in closer to get a better look. She didn't recognize the man.

He walked right up to the door and rang the doorbell as if someone was expecting him. Could it be that the new Mrs. St. Germaine had grown tired of Dominic and found her someone on the side? She could see why the woman would be attracted to this man; he was well built and ruggedly handsome.

Mais, Bianca needed to find out more about this man. This may be just what she needed to get rid of the new Mrs. St. Germaine. She was never good at sharing and wanted him all to herself.

Bianca seriously considered calling Dominic and asking if he was expecting company at the plantation. She could already envision Dominic's reaction if he walked in on his new wife doing the horizontal mambo with another man.

Before picking up the phone, though, she should make sure that the man went inside. Something about the stranger's energy had her unsettled. She watched as the door opened, and Alexis stepped outside. She held her breath and waited for the man to take Alexis in his arms and carry her upstairs. But if she was reading their body language correctly, these two didn't know each other.

She wished she could read lips. He seemed to be asking Alexis something to which she just shook her head. He handed her something and pointed to whatever she was holding. Again, Alexis shook her head. It looked as if the man handed her a business card of some kind and headed back to his car.

Disappointed, Bianca headed back home. She wondered who this man was. He had her curiosity piqued.

Nightfall had descended by the time she made it to the dense woods leading to her small cabin. She preferred to live further away from the others so that when her lover came to visit no one would notice. Although she loved her growing family, she did not want them knowing about her and the Mafia Prince.

She listened as the leaves in the trees rustled from the breeze blowing off of the bayou. She heard something scurrying along the leaves on the ground. She tried to see which creature was lurking about, but the heavy canopy of the branches and foliage above blocked the moonlight from penetrating to illuminate the path to her cabin.

A low moan rose up from the bushes ahead. She took a step back instinctively. An animal did not make that sound. Mais non, she knew exactly what that sound came from. She must see which one made that noise. Who could have broken free?

The closer she got, the louder the moan became. The moans turned into growls. As she neared the thicket of shrubs and trees, the groans and moans abruptly stopped. She gently pushed back a low lying branch that obscured her view.

That was when she saw him. A recently turned zombie was traipsing back and forth moaning as he went. When he turned to her, his eyes were hollow and dry in their sockets.

He stared ahead with all intelligent malice gone; all that remained was an emptiness to him. His skin was already pale and gray as the dead. He had become one of those who walked among the dead. She wondered how this one broke free.

She must get him back to the others before he made his way into town and scared the locals. She couldn't have anyone in town discovering what they did here. A zombie outbreak was the last thing they needed to bring attention to them. As long as she could control them, they were the perfect free labor for the Mafia Prince.

She reached out to the man as he growled viciously at her. The man was still not easy to control. There must be some of his inner soul remaining inside of him. She would have to take care of that.

Chapter 21

Coach William Johnson had been the football coach for this team for over five years now and all had gone well for him. He was one of the top paid football coaches in the south, but he had been in deep with the bookies and the mob for the last four years.

When a bookie came to him four years ago requesting a game be rigged, he brushed him off until he saw the money that would come his way if his team lost. It took little convincing after that discovery. He had controlled the players with no problem, that was until this year. Their new quarterback didn't care about the money he could earn by not passing the ball at the right time or getting sacked by opposing teams. No, all the quarterback cared about was beating a record and making this year a zero loss year. The bookies and the mob Boss didn't want to hear how he couldn't control one player.

This week's game had a lot of money riding on it. If they won, the bookies would begrudgingly pay out a lot of money. If they did have to pay, he would be the one they came looking for, not the quarterback. No, he had to find a way to convince the quarterback it was in his best interest to make the plays his coach gave him. If convincing him didn't work, he would be forced to make sure he didn't play in the upcoming game, or next several games. An injury to his wrist would prevent him from playing.

***

Coach Johnson looked over at his team and explained the night's plays to them. As quarterback Ben Anderson listened to Coach Johnson's pep talk for tonight's game, he suspected that the coach sent the henchmen to his house. They roughed him up until he agreed to throw tonight's game, but he had no evidence to prove it. However, he had a plan, albeit a dangerous one, to find out if Coach Johnson was receiving bribes to lose and win certain games. Why else would the team play well one day and lousy the next? He had seen these men practice, and he knew they were good, or they wouldn't be here, but he couldn't prove that something underhanded was going on. Well, after tonight, he hoped to prove just that. He prayed that he was doing the right thing, though, because this plan could also land him six feet under the ground.

Anderson waited until the second half to put his plan into action. He started off small by changing the game plan just a little as to go easily unnoticed. When they made the touchdown, he noticed the Coach seething on the sidelines, but he couldn't say anything or it would prove that Anderson was right about him. When the moment came for them to get control of the ball, he took it. The throw was perfect, and his teammate caught it masterfully and made another touchdown for the team. This play would be talked about for years to come. It was also the play that sealed Coach Johnson's fate.

***

Coach Johnson was fuming. His quarterback had duped him, and now his team had won the game. It wouldn't be long before the bookies came knocking on his door, wanting to know what happened. The Mafia Prince wouldn't be happy about today either. Of all the damn things to happen to him. He should have pulled Anderson out of the game, especially after making the first touchdown. When they were two touchdowns ahead, he knew the other team wouldn't pull it off; they just weren't that good. Hell, they were basically handing them the game on a silver platter. He had to force the players to hold back, they wanted to open up a case of whoop ass after the bad mouthing the opposing team had done that week. Coach Johnson instructed them to save their strength for next week's game, that game was more important. They all seemed to go for it except for Anderson. Somehow he convinced the other players to listen to him over the course of the day. He was certainly a sneaky little bastard! That was okay; he had some favors he could call in. If he was going to get a visit tonight, then so would the quarterback. He wouldn't be the only one whose career ended today. No, Anderson would pay dearly for this treachery.

Chapter 22

When Rayne Simoneaud saw the help wanted ad for housekeepers at Maison du St. Germaine, she couldn't believe her luck. She hoped the position had flexible hours. She had one year left of school, but her bills were piling up. She filled out several job applications around town, but unless she wanted to work in a strip club or a bar, there weren't too many night jobs. Maybe she would be able to get the hours she needed at Maison du St. Germaine.

As soon as she got out of class, she headed over and filled out a job application. She was hired the next day. She never imagined she would find a job that worked around her crazy class schedule. This year, she took extra hours to finish a semester early.

Rayne had worked at Maison du St. Germaine for over five months. She had never seen a lovelier hotel. The exterior of the hotel was framed with decorative wrought iron and several of the outer rooms also had wrought iron balconies. There was an elegant Victorian garden in the middle of the courtyard that had a cherub fountain in the center. The ambiance here was not only relaxing, but embraced the culture of Louisiana, more specifically New Orleans.

The rooms had absorbed centuries of sounds, smells and emotions of the guests. She considered it an honor to work in this hotel. Despite the fatigue settling into her body, she was anxious to get to work. She loved meeting the various guests that came through these doors. There had been a few that looked down on her, but most guests sincerely wished to share their experiences while visiting this historic city. She loved hearing first hand what people thought of

Bourbon Street, the various voodoo shops around town, the haunted tours, the coffee and especially the food.

The hotel was located near the French Quarter. She wondered if the owner had known how popular this area would be back then. Regardless, it was in a prime location because it wasn't far from the tourist spots. Everything she loved about New Orleans was in walking distance from here. It saddened her when she thought of what was destroyed when Hurricane Katrina hit this region. There had been so much devastation and loss of life. New Orleans was coming back to life, though, and it still had not lost its mystique and intrigue.

She'd heard rumors that the hotel was haunted, but, as of yet, she had not witnessed any hauntings; however, it wouldn't surprise her. If only these walls could talk about the scandals they must have witnessed over the years.

Since working here, she had yet to see the penthouse floor. From what the others said, it was gorgeous. None of the other girls liked to clean that room, though. They said it was always left a mess when they departed. She heard that the only people allowed to stay there were members of the St. Germaine family. Surely someone as rich as this family wouldn't leave the room in complete disarray. When she worked the late night or early morning shift, she noticed a lot of activity going to that floor. She knew better than to ask questions. That could be dangerous in a city such as New Orleans.

While arranging her cart, Mr. Milton, the night manager, walked over to her. She let out an inward groan, "Mr. Milton is there something I can help you with?"

"I just got word that Mr. St. Germaine will be coming to the hotel for an early morning meeting. I need you to go up to the penthouse and make sure that it is clean and orderly before he comes in. I am sure that you are aware that Mr. St. Germaine likes his privacy; I need you to get in and out."

The penthouse took Rayne's breath away. Never in her wildest imagination did she think it would look like this. Unlike the other hotel rooms, it had wood floors that reflected the light from overhead crystal chandeliers that ran throughout the room.

French provincial furniture was expertly placed throughout. The master bedroom had a king size bed that she could get lost in. The master bath was larger than her small apartment.

This place reminded her of when she went to a wealthy person's house to pick up their ironing. Growing up, Rayne's mom would take ironing in at night to earn extra money. The only problem was that her mother had to drive to each of their houses to pick up the laundry.

Rayne's momma did the best she could. Being a single mother was hard enough, but having a mulatto daughter in New Orleans could prove to be extremely difficult. Rayne's momma never would tell her the name of her father. When her mom told her grandmother of her pregnancy, she kicked her out of the house and told her never to come back.

Rayne was studying to become a doctor. She'd inherited her mother's natural instincts as a traiteur. Her mother beamed with pride when she told her that she wanted to be a healer, as well, but Rayne wanted to do this on a more professional basis. She already decided she would open a private practice and not worry if her patients could pay. She would do just like her mother and accept cash or trade. To her, this profession was about healing and not making money.

She looked around the well decorated room, relishing in the things money could buy. The remaining two bedrooms had the same style French provincial furniture. The beds in the suite were canopied. Making sure that no one was here; she lay down on one of the spare beds. It was complete luxury. So this was how the other half lived, she thought to herself. If she closed her eyes, she could imagine herself as a princess.

Shaking herself out of her dream world, she got off of the bed and started cleaning. Looking around, she realized the others were right. Mon Dieu, whoever had been here last had no respect for the beauty of this place. Strewn about were empty liquor bottles and cigar ashes everywhere.

***

Dominic had the beginnings of a migraine and wanted to rest before his next meeting. As Dominic entered his room, he noticed the young woman busy cleaning the penthouse floor. She must be a new hire. He had not seen her face before.

Startled, she gasped when she saw him. Their gazes locked and he felt an immediate attraction to her. She had the most mesmerizing eyes, they were a unique shade of green.

"I am sorry, sir. I was told that you wouldn't be here until later this afternoon."

He waved his hand in the air, "Finish what you are doing. I came earlier than originally planned."

As she hurried to finish up and be out of his way, he imagined what it would be like to have her in bed. The nondescript housekeeping uniform could not hide her voluptuous curves. His hands itched to undress her and see if her body was as beautiful as he imagined.

He shook his head. The way the woman carried herself led him to believe she would not appreciate the way his lustful thoughts were turning.

Chapter 23

He walked quietly to where Bianca was preparing for tonight's ritual. As he neared the small clearing, the sound of beating drums and chanting filled the still night air. The air throbbed with the beat of the batri playing and the ground vibrated with the force of the pounding feet.

A while back, Bianca asked if she could invite several of her voodoo friends from New York to come down and help her perform her black magic. She trusted these people and they would be beneficial in helping her achieve what he wanted. They had slowly made their way down south and set up camp in the back of the plantation. He allowed them to renovate the old slave cabins so that they could live here and stay out of the public's eye.

They had made themselves at home here. They even raised white chickens for their sacrificial rituals. He had seen several priests and priestesses roaming the grounds at night.

As the sound of the drumbeat picked up, he knew the voodoo ritual was about to begin. The pungent smell of burning wood stung his nostrils. The plume of lavender colored smoke rose in the air marking the site of her altar. As he got closer to where the ritual would be performed, he felt the spike of energy that charged the air. His whole body seemed to pulse with the rhythm of the drums. His muscles jumped to the beat of the tambourines, flutes, and rattles.

In the darkness of the night, black candles flickered. Coach William Johnson was secured tightly to the ground by stakes. He would soon learn the risks of gambling and dealing with the Mafia. He laid there unblinking, frozen in fear and watched as the voodoo priestess walked around him chanting. She wore an eerie mask that resembled a human skull, minus the lower jaw and topped with a spray of feathers.

When she spun, it started out slow, but became faster. The dark side of voodoo completely intrigued him. He wondered how she could turn as fast as she did. He wasn't sure if it was even humanly possible to do what she was doing or if some spirit had taken over her body as she suggested.

***

Everything around him seemed to happen in slow motion. He knew his death was near, and he could not stop what was happening to him. If only he could go back in time and play the game honestly. What would the fans say when they learned of his deceit? Would they be able to forgive him for his betrayal? Would his team forgive him for his treachery as well?

As the priestess rubbed a substance on his bare chest, fear trickled down his spine, freezing his very blood. He felt a fire burn deep inside of him as his breathing slowed. Near his head, she shook her ason, a gourd filled with snake vertebrae to honor the Great Serpent spirit who was referred to as Danbala.

Chapter 24

Restless, Alexis walked outside to get some fresh air. Maybe a nice walk would help ease her mind. Lately, she'd had strange dreams. Some mornings she swore it was as if she hadn't slept at all.

As she walked by the riverbank, a sudden gust of cold wind blew over her. She wrapped her arms around herself to ward off the chill. She looked out over the river.

As she headed back towards the house, she stopped and listened intently. She thought she heard something behind her. She looked around and shook off the eerie feeling of being watched. Then a movement in the woods caught her eye and panic took over. Was someone out there? No, that couldn't be possible. It had to be a woodland creature, probably a deer roaming the woods.

She took in a deep breath and tried to calm her nerves. She was being silly. No one was lurking about. Why would someone want to come onto the property? She was letting those questions the private investigator asked her scare her.

She couldn't imagine Dominic being involved with any missing girls. He had been taught to respect women, and he would never harm a female. He was too gentle and loving with her to do something as monstrous as what the private investigator suggested.

****

As Bianca watched Alexis walk along the riverbank, something dark and sinister came over her. If only she could confront her with the things she did with her husband. Bianca had to bite her tongue to keep from calling out to Alexis. She had played this scene out in her head so many times, but instead of doing anything that could harm her relationship with Dominic, Bianca watched as Alexis gazed out into the water.

Jealousy filled every pore in Bianca's body. Alexis always seemed to dress to perfection, and her clothes fit her like a glove. Bianca understood why Dominic had to marry this woman, but that didn't help with the jealous feelings that took over Bianca every time she saw the woman.

This woman would be in the shop tomorrow for a reading. She considered telling her that she suspected her husband was cheating on her, but that would only upset HIM and she did not want that.

***

After eating dinner, Alexis headed to their bedroom to get ready for Dominic to come home. While out earlier today, she'd picked up a new nightgown and wanted to see what he thought of it. She took a nice warm bubble bath and slipped into her new nightgown. It was an emerald green that matched her eyes to perfection.

The fitted bodice showed off her voluptuous breasts. The lustrous fabric was finely cut and flattering to her figure. She paid more for it than she had ever even paid for a dress, but as soon as she saw it, she had to have it; besides, Dominic could afford it.

She stepped in front of the mirror and turned in several directions to make sure that the gown flattered her as much as she thought it did in the shop. She felt outrageously sexy in the outfit and couldn't wait for Dominic to get home.

As soon as Dominic walked into the bedroom, she saw the desire in his eyes. "Cher you look exquisite."

Alexis needed no further prompting; she ran into his waiting arms. "I wanted to look nice for you."

Nibbling on her ear, he whispered, "I love the nightgown, but you look better out of it."

He pulled her to him and lifted her mouth to his. He flicked his tongue over her teeth before deepening his kiss. She slid her body against his. Her body was assaulted with electrical pulsations throughout as his hands roamed over it.

She slipped her hands under his shirt and ran them over the expanse of his back. He cupped her bottom and pulled her tight against his body.

As her nightgown fell to the floor, he brushed a thumb over the peak of her breast. She instinctively arched into him as desire built inside of her.

His clothes came off with ease as he carried her off to the bed. He lowered his head and took a nipple into his mouth while caressing her other breast. Incredible sensations exploded like fireworks in her body as his mouth traveled over it.

He continued to massage the most sensitive of her parts until the pleasure turned to swells of tortuous bliss. He carried her higher and higher until she convulsed against his hand. At the peak of her orgasm, he thrust deep inside of her, taking her to another plane of complete stimulation.

She grasped his powerful hips to bring him deeper inside of her. He kissed her with such passion; his tongue plunged into her mouth as he took her harder. They took complete pleasure as each stroke brought on another tremor of an orgasm. As she cried out his name and shuddered against him, she felt Dominic thrust deep inside of her and find his release as well.

***

No sooner than Alexis had left the shop, her mysterious visitor from the other day walked into the store.   Could he be following Alexis? If so, why?

This man was breathtakingly handsome with skin the color of warm caramel, a chiseled jaw and the most mesmerizing eyes. Her grandmother would have called them voodoo eyes since they changed with the mood. He screamed danger as well. This man may be what she needed to get Dominic jealous.

Bianca tucked a strand of her unruly hair behind her ear and looked directly into the man's eyes, "Is there something I can help you with today?"

Could this man be one of Dominic's new enemies? Why was he trying to gather information? Could he be a voodoo priest sizing up the competition? Did he know what she had been up to and come to confront her? She shook her head and dismissed that thought. Why would he come in here? No one knew that she secretly worked for the Mafia Prince.

He approached her with an outstretched hand, "Bonjour, my name is Guy Mayon. Would you take a look at a picture and tell me if you have seen this girl?"

Bianca took the picture and looked at it. She tried to hide any emotion. If this man were asking about this girl, it could mean trouble for them, "I see so many people that I am honestly not sure. Is she missing or something?"

He took the picture from Bianca, "Her bank statement showed that she had purchased something from your store the day before she went missing, and I am just trying to trace her last steps."

Bianca shook her head, "I really do wish I could help you, but like I said, so many people come in and out of here that I can't keep track of their faces."

He pulled out a business card and handed it to her, "Well, if you happen to remember anything, please call me. Her family is concerned about her, and they have asked that I help find her for them."

Bianca wet her lips and stared at the business card. This man was a private investigator. If he did start to cause them trouble it should be easy enough to get rid of him.

Chapter 25

Since moving to New Orleans, Teresa Scarcelli had come to love this town. It took a while for it to grow on her, but now the very pulse of it beat in her body. She had been studying more and more of the city's unique history and came across a lot of information about a voodoo queen named Marie Laveau. Learning more about this intriguing woman had almost become an obsession with her.

From everything she had learned, Marie Laveau was an extraordinary woman. She was not only a voodoo priestess, but an extremely successful one that could do both good and black magic. Marie Laveau was a descendant from foremothers who served the voodoo deities. The combination of her spiritual powers, clairvoyance, healing abilities, beauty and charisma made her a shrewd business woman who assumed the role of leadership of a multiracial community along with accumulating wealth and property. Her influence extended to every segment of New Orleans society, from slaves to the upper-class. It was said that she controlled several people in very prominent roles through magic or blackmail. These people included policemen, judges and city officials.

According to legend, Marie Laveau was the daughter of a wealthy white planter and his mulatto mistress. It was believed that at the time of her death in 1881, she had been nearly one hundred years old. As with all tales, there were rumors attached to them. It was rumored that her daughter, named Marie II, wanted to give the impression that the Queen of Voodoo reigned just as beautiful as ever and secretly took her place. It had been said both mother and daughter could use voodoo's magical powers to control lovers, acquaintances and enemies.

Rumors were whispered around New Orleans about secret rituals held deep in the bayous. It was even believed that a portion of the worshippers were caucasian. They were believed to join in on the rituals in the hope of obtaining a desired power. Possibly to win back a lost love, to obtain a new lover, or to even eliminate a business associate or enemy.

It had even been rumored that Marie Laveau found beautiful black or mulatto women for wealthy white men seeking a mistress or two. Marie Laveau's Creole boudoirs helped her gain notoriety with her unique flair for voodoo. It was said she had a considerable knowledge of spells and would take money to help a public official win an election or make a love potion for a wealthy white woman. She would help blacks with no charge for services. It soon became fashionable to come to Marie Laveau for a reading. Teresa had a feeling a lot of the tales were exaggerated, but she found some documentation to support several of the rumors.

From her research, she found out that Marie's daughter continued running the Maison Blanche, White House. This establishment provided clandestine meetings between white men and young black women along with voodoo practices without having to fear it would be raided by the police. It was whispered that the police feared retribution if they ever crossed Marie.

Teresa was meandering down Bourbon Street, searching for a voodoo shop. Her mind wandered as she thought of all the things she could do with voodoo.

She may be able to help her mom rid herself of her abusive husband faster than she anticipated. Voodoo may speed up the process. Her skin tingled in anticipation of their plan finally coming together. If only it could happen now, but it was not in the cards at this moment. She still had a lot to accomplish before she could prove that a woman could run the Family.

Teresa learned that there had been white Voodoo priestesses, but not too many. From her research, she learned that a traiteur was normally a Cajun who practiced voodoo. Now she just had to find someone who could teach her the practices she wanted to learn.

Chapter 26

Rayne Simoneaud found herself in a difficult situation. She had been having an affair with a married man for several months and now she was pregnant. When she played around with a love potion that would make him attracted to her, she never once believed that it would work, but no sooner than she said the spell, he came to her.

She was not ready to have a child, but could not find it in herself to abort the child. Killing a child, born or unborn, was not in her nature.

She had to tell the father. She would not be able to hide the fact she was pregnant any longer. She was already showing. She planned to tell him he had nothing to worry about; that she would give the child up for adoption. At first she'd found her lover intriguing, but lately she sensed a dark side to him. She met him while working at the hotel and felt the attraction to him instantly. Shy as she was, she still attracted the bad boys and never someone she could build a life with. As it stood, she needed to go away and hide out for a while until the baby came. Even though New Orleans was a big town, her family was still tight knit. They would ask questions, questions she didn't want to answer. Her family would want her to keep the baby, offering to help raise it, but that was not what she wanted. She was still young and hadn't accomplished any of the goals she set for herself. No, this baby would be better off with a family that could provide for it, someone who would love it unconditionally. This child growing inside of her needed a mother and father to love it. That was not something she could give it now. She had planned to break it off with her lover, but since she hadn't seen him in a few weeks, she hadn't had a chance to end it and now this. This wasn't something she could write in a letter and send to him. No, she should tell him in person.

***

Rayne bolted upright in bed; unsure of exactly what woke her. She let out a scream when she saw the man. "Please, please don't hurt me. Take whatever you want from the house, but don't hurt me."

Instead of listening to her, he moved closer to the bed, ready to pounce. She pleaded with him one more time, "Please, I am pregnant. Don't hurt my baby."

He sneered at her, "Lady, that baby is the whole reason I am here."

Dread seeped into her bones. Why would he do this to her? She told him he didn't have to worry about the baby, that she didn't want him to leave his wife for her. She'd talked to several adoption agencies and found one she was comfortable with. The agency already had a family in mind, one that didn't care that the baby was of a mixed race. Besides, you had to look close to see that she came from a biracial family. Her hazel eyes, which had a tendency to be more green than anything else, tended to throw people off. She was always being told that she had voodoo eyes, which were in her blood. That was what made her a good traiteur. Now, she would never be able to show the world that she was just as good of a traiteur as her mother and her child would never see the light of day.

When the man went to reach for her, she fought back with all of her strength. She was determined not to go down without a fight. She scratched and bit at him as he tried to restrain her. She managed to rake her nails across his face, leaving a gouge mark. He picked up his revolver and struck her against her head with the butt of his gun.

With blood running down her face, she glared at him, "I will not forget this. He did not have to send someone to hurt me or my baby."

***

A shudder made its way down his spine as she continued to glare at him. He hoped his Boss knew what he was doing. This woman looked as if she could put a spell on them. He had never believed in all that hocus pocus until his dealings with the voodoo priestess. Now, since he knew for sure this stuff existed, he preferred to observe it from behind the scenes.

By the time he had her arms and legs bound with the rope, she was hysterical and muttering to herself. He didn't know what she was saying, but he had a feeling it was not good. She continued to struggle to free herself from the ropes that securely bound her. When he picked her up and threw her over his shoulder, the screams became almost unbearable. He looked over at his partner, "Grab something to cram in this one's mouth to shut her up."

The partner looked through her dresser drawers and found a pair of socks to stuff in her mouth. To make sure she didn't spit them out, he also grabbed a pair of nylon stockings to tie around her mouth to hold the socks in place.

The silver moon was hidden in the starless night. Even the night must know that evil lurked about. The small boat quietly puttered down the bayou on the way to see the voodoo woman as directed by their Boss.

The two men pulled up to the clearing that was made from the frequent stops lately. The bayou was calm tonight and the water gently lapped against the small boat and bayou's edge. The small gas engine was the only sound out this evening. Even the mosquitoes seemed to leave them alone.

The murky smell of the bayou overpowered their senses in this spot. As soon as the larger one stepped out of the boat, his foot sank into the muddy water. He let out a muttered curse as he tried to shake off the mud from his boots. He listened to make sure no one else was about. All he heard was the semiconscious lady in the boat softly moaning. He looked down at the young woman who had caused so much trouble for him tonight. Her sheer nightgown left nothing to the imagination. The humidity of the night had the fabric clinging to all the right curves. Her pregnant belly was just starting to show. She fought like a banshee when they broke into her house tonight, trying to protect the life growing inside of her. Dried blood crusted over her face where he'd hit her with the butt of his revolver. The Boss told them in no uncertain terms that they must bring the woman alive to the voodoo priestess. He wanted her to deal with this one. This was one time Brian had no problem letting the voodoo woman deal with eliminating the Boss's problem. This woman was unsettling. Even in the darkness of the night, her green eyes glowed with her hatred for them.

They must hurry and get her to the voodoo priestess. The Boss told them that this was a special request from someone that could help their business immensely. But he wondered if the Boss wasn't the one who needed this done and he didn't want to let the voodoo priestess know that he had dipped his wick in someone else. The Boss and voodoo priestess never showed any display of intimacy in front of them, but there was a chemistry there that led him to believe the two were hot and heavy. He had worked for the Boss long enough to know the man couldn't keep it in his pants. He doubted either the wife or voodoo priestess knew, or the man wouldn't have a pecker.

He looked at his partner, "Come on. Let's get this over with."

He hoisted the woman over his shoulder, mindful of her swollen belly. The partner watched him shift the weight, "I am still not sure about this. I sure hope the Boss knows what he is doing."

Brian looked back at the man, "Shut up you fool. You don't want the Boss to know you are questioning his orders, you hear me."

He waved his hands in the air, "I am not questioning his orders. This whole thing gives me the creeps is all."

"The voodoo priestess will take care of her. We are just the delivery boys." Even though Brian spoke the words, he didn't truly believe them. Usually, the boss let him handle these things on his own, but he'd asked Brian to train this recruit to see if he could indeed be trusted. If this guy were the mole, they would soon know.

As they walked onto the porch of the small shack, the door opened and the voodoo priestess pointed to the couch. "Put her on the couch for now. We will begin soon."

He dropped the woman on the couch, unceremoniously. The voodoo priestess walked over to the woman and looked her directly in the eyes. They both looked at each other in shock. Even Brian did a double take at the two standing so near. There was definitely a resemblance that he had not noticed before; they both had the same eyes and facial features.

***

The voodoo priestess took a deep breath and instantly knew why he wanted her disposed of. Indignation rippled through her body as his deception became evident.

Rayne looked at the woman with contempt in her eyes. The voodoo priestess murmured something out loud as she continued her scrutiny of the woman. Even with fire in her eyes, hair unkempt, torn and bloody clothes, the voodoo priestess could see the woman's inner beauty, something she did not have. Suddenly, the young lady started rocking back and forth on the couch and then she began hissing. The voodoo priestess stared at her. How did she know about voodoo and curses? The voodoo priestess reached into her shirt to touch the Gris Gris bag she kept safely hidden near her breast. Let this woman spit out curses; they would do her no harm. She looked at the two men who brought the woman here and walked over to the small altar she had in her home. Grabbing two Gris Gris bags, she informed them, "Keep these on you at all times. They will protect you from what this one is spouting off. Do not let anyone else touch it and keep it near your skin to keep you safe."

Brian didn't have to be told twice as he stuck it in the waistband of his jeans. His partner watched in utter confusion, but he did as Brian; he did not want to be the one killed by some vengeful woman's curse.

The voodoo priestess picked up her zombie potion and applied it to the woman's exposed skin. The two men watched as the young woman's ranting became slower until she stopped altogether. She slumped forward, but Brian knew from experience this one wasn't dead.

The voodoo priestess looked at the two men and informed them, "Bring her to the boat and drown her in the bayou. I don't want her to join the other workers. No, this one is too strong willed." Bianca didn't want this baby born. She knew exactly whose baby it was and she would deal with his betrayal in her own way. He thought he could be devious and tell her it was for someone else. How dare he think he could fool her! When the time was right, she would show him how powerful she really was, but for now she would abide by his wishes.

***

The two men loaded the now comatose young woman back onto the boat. Before heading out, Brian added two concrete bricks to the boat. "I want to make sure this one sinks to the bottom of the bayou. There is no way I want to make either the Boss or that voodoo woman mad. Plus, this one tried to put a hex on us. We don't want her coming after us."

His partner shook his head, "I don't feel right about this. I have never killed a pregnant woman before, much less one that is a voodoo woman."

Brian informed him, "I don't think she is a voodoo woman, but she knows enough about the subject to put a hurt on us. I for one don't plan on taking this Gris Gris bag off."

As they headed to the bend in the bayou to dump the body, the young woman sat upright and let out a hideous laugh, causing both men to jump up in fear. Brian never had a zombie come back to life before, so he grabbed his gun and shot her. Instead of dying, she glared at the two men and started chanting. Her voice sounded like a snake's hiss instead of human. She then told the men, "If I can't have any more children, then neither shall the two of you or your Boss. Tell him that he will never sire a child."

Brian grabbed the young woman and threw her overboard. Her body made a loud splash as it hit the water. His partner grabbed the concrete blocks that they had secured to her feet earlier and threw them overboard as well. As she met her maker in the muddy waters of the bayou, both men said a prayer that they were rid of her once and for all.

Brian looked at his partner, "Man, she just may be voodoo."

The other man made sure that his Gris Gris bag was still tucked securely in his waistband. "I am not about to tell the Boss that she put a curse on him."

Brian nodded in agreement, "Hell no, mon ami." He turned the boat back around, "Let's get the hell out of here and never mention this to anyone."

"That is fine with me. Do you put up with this creepy shit all the time?"

Brian shook his head, "Mais non! Nothing like this has ever happened to me before." Brian was one of the Boss's top enforcers and he planned on staying that way. He had no plans of telling him what happened here. Hopefully, this new guy kept his trap shut too. If not, it could cause some serious problems. The Boss didn't like when things went wrong, and this was about as wrong as one could get as far as he was concerned. Hell, he shot the woman and she kept on chanting. He had seen some weird shit lately, but this one took the cake. He knew he shot her in the heart and she should have died on the spot. Instead, no blood flowed from the gunshot wound and she continued chanting. He hoped she didn't pick up the heavy bricks and walk out of the bayou.

Chapter 27

William Chaisson looked around his office in disgust. The office was cleaned that morning and it was a complete mess again. Books and papers were scattered about as he had spent most of the day and into the night researching and drafting motions.

Truth be told; he was hiding from the Mafia Prince and his hired goon. He should never have gone into the poker room the other night. But, his day had been bad and he needed to relieve the stress. He thought a hand or two of poker would help, but before he had realized it, he was down twenty thousand dollars and the Mafia Prince gave him until today to pay.

The personal injury case William was counting on to settle the debt didn't seem to be coming to his rescue. His client wasn't happy with the offer the insurance company made and declined it outright saying she knew she could get more. William ruefully shook his head and began to realize that the offer was slipping through his hands along with his chance to pay his debt. No matter how hard he tried to get the woman to see reason, she believed her case was worth more money. Hell, she hadn't even been injured in the car accident; she should be happy that the insurance company offered her thirty thousand just to make the case go away. Their client was in the wrong. He was drunk when he rear ended his client. But now his client saw dollar signs. William didn't see that happening; especially, since the insurance company had informed him they would take their chances in court. Mais non, they would not give him another settlement offer.

Her damn greed more than likely sealed his fate. These goons would probably break his legs, if not worse.

After locking the office door behind him, he walked up the dark staircase that led to his apartment. His footsteps echoed in the stairway. As with most houses and businesses here in downtown New Orleans, his office was downstairs and he lived above it. As he made his way upstairs, he looked around waiting to see if someone emerged from the shadows.

He opened his door and walked into the darkened area. The two bedroom and two bath apartment had a full size kitchen and a living room that looked over the French Quarter. There wasn't much of a dining room, but since he spent little time eating here, it didn't bother him. He didn't think the kitchen had ever been used. He preferred to get his coffee at the little café right down the street and, generally, he ordered takeout or ate at one of the fine restaurants that New Orleans had to offer. His refrigerator was usually bare. He kept a few things in the pantry, but that was mainly snack food. He led the perfect bachelor life and planned to keep it that way.

As soon as he walked into the master bedroom, his apprehension grew. The sliding door that led to the deck was open. Before he could leave the apartment, the intruder knocked him unconscious.

***

Officers Boudreaux and Brusly watched the road ahead as they waited for a speeder or drunk driver to come their way. So far, the road had remained deserted and dark; not a soul was out.

Brusly asked, "So where do you think everyone is? I can't believe that it is this dead."

"Man, I thought for sure this full moon would keep us busy, but damn, everyone seems to be keeping off the road tonight."

"I hate just sitting here waiting for something to happen."

"It doesn't look like anything is happening anywhere. Everybody must be tired or something. This sucks big time."

Brusly couldn't agree more. Normally, the streets would be busy with tourists, conventioneers or drunks, but for some reason, no one was out having a good time. "I wish Sheriff Renault would let us patrol instead of just sitting here and waiting for someone to drive by. We would catch more speeders and drunks if we could patrol." At least when they patrolled, they weren't so damn bored.

Boudreaux replied, "The town council is complaining about the amount of gas wasted when we patrol; so, we have to sit here in the dark. Hell, we have to sit out here with the windows cracked and not run the engine to conserve gas. If they had to do this for just an hour they would change their minds pretty damn quick."

"Mais, they only think about themselves and not us poor working stiffs."

As Brusly picked up his phone, he saw the headlights barreling down on them, "Mon ami, we have one coming right for us."

The two officers watched in disbelief as the car flew right past them and never slowed down for the hairpin curve.

Officer Boudreaux exclaimed, "Mon Dieu, he is going to go straight into the river."

With their lights flashing and siren blaring, they pursued the driver to, hopefully, catch his attention before he killed himself.

***

William Chaisson felt as if he was flying. It never even dawned on him that his car was out of control when it started to flip. The world around him moved in slow motion. His world was suddenly right side up and then upside down, but it all went unrecognized by him. He never noticed how many times the car flipped. The sound of crunching metal didn't phase him. The sound was all that filled the night air as the officers watched in horror as the car careened into the murky river water.

The car landed upside down in the Mississippi River. Glass rained down on his head as the water rushed into the car. He hung upside down by his seatbelt, completely dazed and disoriented. He was in a dreamlike state of mind. He could hear and see what went on around him, but it did not register in his mind. He couldn't even move. Was he dead? Did his soul just not know to leave his body?

He tried to shout out, hoping that someone would help him, but he couldn't find his voice. Surely, someone must have seen the accident; New Orleans was always busy.

"We need to hurry in case someone is alive down there," the young officer called to his partner. "This was unlike any accident I have ever seen. There is no way the driver survived."

Diving into the murky water, the officer forced the car door open and pulled out the injured man from the submerged car. The officer informed his partner, "He doesn't appear to be alive."

Somewhere through the fog in his brain, he listened in horror to what the man said. He couldn't be dead; could he? He desperately tried to correct the officer. When he went to speak, his mouth refused to cooperate. How could he be dead when he felt the excruciating pain and heard every word they said?

He felt himself being moved into the ambulance. The bright lights flashing in the night sky hurt his eyes. Someone was checking his vitals. Good, then they would know he was alive. The person taking his vitals was talking, but he couldn't make out a word they were saying. The world around him became distorted. Maybe he was dead after all?

Suddenly, white hot pain took over his whole body. He tried to scream out, but his mouth still refused to cooperate.

Chapter 28

Bianca had been waiting for the opportunity to practice on a voodoo doll in public. For this particular voodoo doll, she convinced the dry cleaner Mason Arnault used into selling her one of his shirts. She paid the dry cleaner handsomely for the shirt. Mason probably never noticed a shirt missing. He had plenty there for her to choose from.

She also paid the barber, Harvey Ortego, extra money to save her a lock of hair from Mason Arnault. Harvey was the barber that all the prestigious men here used. Since moving back home, she had been paying him to save hair clippings for her voodoo dolls. She also made the same request with another beautician. It added an authenticity to the dolls that her customers demanded. Now, if the person whose hair she used suffered some ill effects it was a bonus for her. It meant that her powers were strengthening.

Bianca studied Mason Arnault's movements these last few days to ascertain the best time to try her plan. The man was habitual to say the least. Every day he walked into Café Orleans at seven o'clock in the morning and ordered the same thing; a café au lait with skim milk and a beignet, hold the powdered sugar. He may say he was trying to cut back all he wanted, but his buttons were at their breaking point. At any minute, Bianca felt that one would break free and ricochet across the café.

She arrived at the coffee shop fifteen minutes early. After she ordered her café au lait and beignets with powdered sugar, she found a seat in the back corner of the café. She needed to stay hidden as much as possible, but she still wanted to be near to witness this first hand.

Once settled at the table, she placed her large purse on her lap so that she could easily maneuver the voodoo doll while keeping it out of the patrons' sight. A sinister smile formed across her face when he entered the café. She waited for him to place his order and sit down before playing with him.

She started off with something simple. Bianca took some powdered sugar and dropped it onto the front of the doll's pants. She watched in amazement as Mason became annoyed with sugar on his pants. He brushed them off the best he could and surveyed the table to see where the sugar came from. She let out a soft giggle when he picked up his beignet and not only looked at it, but shook it against the napkin to see if there was any sugar on it.

Next, she picked up her straight pen and poked him in the shoulder. He winced and grabbed his shoulder. This was working better than she'd imagined.

She took the pin and jabbed him in the back, harder this time. She could barely control her joy when he gasped and reached for his back. Yes, this would work.

Mason Arnault got up to leave. Before he left, there was one more experiment she wanted to try. She took the voodoo doll in her hands, grasped one arm firmly and removed the arm. She watched in amazement as Mason Arnault's arm fell to the ground as he walked out the door. He immediately howled in pain as blood gushed out from the spot where his arm had been attached to his body.

Bianca was quite pleased with herself. Her powers were definitely strengthening. She couldn't wait to share her findings and see who to make a voodoo doll of next. With this new torture added to their arsenal, they could make their enemies' deaths quick, or slow and painful. He could do various things to his enemies' bodies without being near them. All she needed was a lock of their hair and a piece of clothing.

Chapter 29

Bianca was busy working in the shop when she saw a figure walk by the front window. She stopped in mid-sentence while talking to a customer and looked out dumbfounded. "This can't be," she thought to herself.

Bianca stepped out into the hot, humid air and watched as the lost soul walked the streets of New Orleans. She watched in horror as several people stepped out of the man's way and gasped as he passed by them.

Her customer walked out of the store. "That is an evil Diablo at work." She made a sign of the cross and spat on the sidewalk. "Mais, there is some powerful black magic at work."

Bianca nodded in disbelief. She needed to make her and the Mafia Prince a powerful Gris Gris bag to wear. But first she must call the Mafia Prince and let him know what was going on. Word would soon reach him either way. It would be better to have the news come from her.

***

Just a few shops down, Ian Landry was bringing out café au laits and beignets to his customers when he suddenly dropped the tray to the ground. The customer jumped up in surprise, "What the hell man. You look as if you have seen a ghost."

Ian quickly apologized, "I am so sorry. Let me get this cleaned up, and I will be right out with some more." As Ian cleaned up the mess, he watched as the man strolled down Bourbon Street as if he didn't have a care in the world.

As Ian stood up from cleaning the mess, the man turned around. A chill swept across Ian. He stared back at Ian with eyes as black as night. Ian couldn't explain it, but it was almost as if it was only a shell of the man walking these streets. His face looked as if it had aged fifty years and there was no color to his skin.

Mrs. Danielle Melancon came up behind Ian and let out a surprised gasp, "I thought the newspaper said that William Chaisson died. Isn't his funeral tomorrow?"

All Ian could do was nod.

Mrs. Danielle Melancon exclaimed, "Mais that can't be William Chaisson. He looks years older. It has to be a relative of his in town for his funeral."

He looked intently at the man on the street. It sure looked like him, but she was right; it was an older version of the man. But the man held an uncanny resemblance to him.

***

The Mafia Prince had never wanted to silence his phone before in his life, but right now he wanted to throw the damn thing out the window. He has received repeated calls from various people wanting to know if he'd heard about William Chaisson.

It had to be someone else. He witnessed Bianca give the man the drugs and the car go into the river. He even had the damn coroner confirm that William Chaisson was dead and scheduled to be buried. So why was the man walking down Bourbon Street as if nothing was wrong? Where did the man get the balls to do that in front of him?

Surely, the man couldn't be that daft as to walk boldly around town knowing the Mafia Prince had a hit on him.

***

Detective Mike Bailey had been with the New Orleans Police Department going on fifteen years now. After finishing his tour in the Navy Seals, he joined the police force. It just so happened that when he left the Navy, he was stationed in New Orleans and fell in love with the area, wanting to stay. He couldn't picture working anywhere else.

As soon as he reached his desk, his phone rang, "Bailey."

He listened to what the dispatcher said and rolled his eyes upward. Of all the asinine calls he had gotten over the last few months, this one took the cake. The dispatcher had received numerous reports of a dead guy, more importantly, William Chaisson, walking along Bourbon Street. Mais, all the motier foux, crazies, were out today, and it was not even a full moon.

Bailey didn't bother to call his partner and let him know about the call. He and his wife had gone to get a quick bite to eat. There was no reason to call him in for something like this.

Because of traffic and the commotion the sighting of William Chaisson was causing, it took longer than normal to get to Bourbon Street. On the way there, he called the funeral home to confirm they weren't missing a body.

"Crescent City Funeral Home, how may I help you?"

"This is Detective Mike Bailey with the New Orleans Police Department. We are receiving numerous prank calls this afternoon, and I am hoping to put this fire out quickly. Can you please confirm that you do, in fact, have William Chaisson's body there, and it is ready for the funeral?"

The young girl let out a low moan. He was beginning to regret making this call, "Well, sir, my boss is on the line with your department to report the robbery. It seems as if the mortician was preparing the body for the funeral when he had to step away for a bit. He wasn't feeling too well, I guess. He went to the bathroom, but didn't see a problem with leaving the body. It's not like we have ever had problems in the past with bodies being stolen or just walking off."

"So, let me make sure I have this right. You are saying that William Chaisson's body is missing?"

"Yes, sir, that is exactly what I am saying. I will tell you the same thing I told my boss. I never left my desk this morning and never saw anyone walk towards the back. I sure didn't see someone leave with a body. There is a window that they could have gone through and there is also the back door, but it was locked. From what we can tell, it doesn't look like someone broke in. It is almost as if the man just woke up and left."

Detective Bailey shook his head. This couldn't be good. Son of a bitch, who would steal a body from a funeral home and why?

He finally made it to Bourbon Street and parked on the side of the road. If this turned out to involve William Chaisson, the city officials would want answers. No one liked when one of the city's elite was killed in a car accident much less the body got stolen and left on Bourbon Street.

As he neared the man who aimlessly wandered the street, he became frozen in place. If that wasn't William Chaisson, it could be his identical twin. The only difference was this man looked much older than William Chaisson. His pallor had a gray tint to it which could be because the man had been dead for a couple of days now.

As Bailey moved in to apprehend the man, he lunged for the detective. Jumping back quickly, he reached for his gun. He didn't want to discharge his weapon in public, so he kept his gun pointed on the man while reaching for his taser gun.

***

Bianca watched this play out in front of her in complete horror. Before the police had arrived on scene, she'd cast a spell on a voodoo doll and she hoped this worked. If this wasn't the hair of William Chaisson, she would kill another person in an instant. Without hesitation, she grabbed the voodoo doll and ripped it in half. The crowd was too heavy for her to see if it worked, but all of a sudden, she heard screaming and people rushing back towards her shop. If the reaction of the crowd could be used to judge the effectiveness of her spell, then she'd managed to kill William Chaisson.

This wasn't what Dominic wanted. He wanted the man to watch as he was buried alive. He wanted his death to be slow, but that wasn't the case this time. How did the man wake up and walk out of the funeral home?

She picked up the phone and called the Mafia Prince, "It is done. He died quicker than you originally wanted, but I couldn't allow him to walk around the streets of New Orleans. Plus the cops had arrived, and they were going to gun him down. The end result could have been bad."

***

He had to agree. The last thing they needed was for people to realize that zombies walked around out there. He would have to watch his voodoo priestess closer. This was not the first time one of her spells had gone awry, and he wanted to make sure that this didn't continue to happen.

***

Detective Bailey looked at the carnage in horror. How the hell did the man suddenly split in half? It happened so quickly; he didn't even realize what had transpired at first. Now, there was blood everywhere. He looked around and noticed that it didn't take long for the crowd to disperse.

He picked up the phone and called the crime scene techs as well as the coroner's office. This time he wanted fingerprints taken so that he could personally verify this was William Chaisson. The family confirmed the body the last time, but this time he wanted definite proof this was Chaisson.

Could it be that someone messed up, and Chaisson wasn't dead? It was rumored that Chaisson owed the wrong people a lot of money, and they were threatening to collect at any moment. Did he fake his death the first time and they found out? Did they finally locate him and make good on their promise?

But how could they get to him with so many witnesses around? It was as if someone tore the body in half.

By the time Bailey arrived back to the precinct from the earlier fiasco, he had a headache. He stopped by the vending machine and grabbed a bag of chips and soda. This may not provide the nourishment he needed, but at least it would put something in his stomach so he could finish his report and go home. Right now, he wanted a cold beer and mindless television.

As he prepared to leave, he noticed Officer Aucoin heading his way, "Sir, we have a positive match on the fingerprints. There is no doubt about it, your dead man this afternoon was William Chaisson. We still don't know what happened at the funeral home. Several of the crime scene techs are headed that way to go sweep the area to search for clues."

"Keep me apprised of the situation then."

"Yes, sir."

As Bailey walked out the door, he thought about the case and how strange this all was. As he unlocked his car door, his phone rang once again. This time it was his friend, Guy Mayon, calling. Guy was a former police detective who had tired of the politics and dirty cops; he left the force and started working for himself. He mainly took on missing persons cases, but would take on anything that helped pay the bills as well. There were times he considered taking Guy up on his offer to join him, but for now, he would stick with the police force. "My man, how is it going?"

Guy asked, "Busy. Mon ami, are you up to meeting at The Oyster House for dinner and conversation?"

"I don't know, man; it has been a long day and I am tired."

Guy persisted, "I am buying. I need to talk to you about a few things that have come up lately."

"Okay. I am leaving the station now."

"I will meet you there. If you make it there before me, grab us a quiet table."

Now Bailey's curiosity was piqued, "Okay, but like I told you before, I am tired tonight."

Guy let out a chortle, "When I tell you what I have, I don't think you will be tired anymore."

The Oyster House was one of the best seafood restaurants here in New Orleans. It may not have the same dining experience as the upscale restaurants, but it had some damn fine food. Downtown was busier than normal at this hour and he had to park a few blocks away. The sidewalks were crowded with locals and vacationing tourists alike, all taking their time to get to where they were going. If it was this busy right now, he dreaded when Mardi Gras came around. The crowds of people would be overwhelming, and if you stood still long enough, they would swallow you whole.

By the time Bailey made it to the restaurant, Guy was already there. They ordered their food and chatted over a beer. Bailey could tell that Guy had something significant to say, but he was taking his sweet time. After the waitress had delivered their food, he asked, "Okay Guy, what the hell is so important that you had to buy me supper?"

Guy let out a sigh, "I hear that you had an interesting case this afternoon."

Bailey chucked, "Is that what this is about? I did have a strange case, but I'm sure once we look into everything it will be easily explained. The one thing I do know is that William Chaisson is most definitely dead now."

Guy took a swig of his beer before continuing, "But what if he was dead to begin with?"

Bailey looked at him dumbfounded, "You have been drinking the water around here too long. There is no such thing as all this voodoo mumbo jumbo. I think William Chaisson faked his death and then when whoever he owed money to found out, they hunted him down and killed him."

"William Chaisson owed the wrong people money, but I also have a feeling that they killed him and turned him into the walking dead, before today."

Bailey shook his head, "I saw him walking the streets of New Orleans this afternoon. Trust me; he was breathing before he was sliced in half. I still haven't figured out how the hell that happened. Crime scene techs are still combing the area for clues."

"What about how the coroner swore that it was Chaisson that he had in his morgue earlier. Even the family swore Chaisson died days ago."

"I can't explain that. Maybe the family mistook the dead body for that of William Chaisson earlier. There was no autopsy. His blood alcohol level came back way over the limits. It was a drunk driving accident that ended in grave consequences. Maybe, William put another body in the car, hoping it would be burned beyond recognition. I don't know, I can't explain that. We are still looking into all the details."

"What would you say if I told you I am investigating several strange cases just like the one you witnessed today? There have been reports of people walking aimlessly around New Orleans, and now there are several women who've disappeared around town as well."

Bailey looked at his friend, "Please don't tell me you are buying into all this hype about zombies?"

Guy shook his head, "No, I do not believe brain eating zombies are invading New Orleans, but I do believe something strange is going on. There are too many reports floating around out there and then there are also an increasing number of reports on missing girls. I believe we may have a human trafficking ring here in New Orleans."

"What makes you suspect that?"

"I have received calls from several parents requesting that I look into their daughter's disappearance. When I called the precinct to ask for their files, I was shown the door. I expected to be given the runaround, but not the door."

Bailey ran his hand on his chin while he thought, "That is strange. You are ex-police; they should treat you differently. Why don't you give me the names and I will look into it? You know for a fact that the girls were reported missing."

"Mais oui. The parents gave me the officer's name that they spoke with and the missing person's report number. I can't get any information when I call though. When they try to call, they also get the runaround."

A chill of apprehension ran through Bailey. He'd suspected for some time that there were some dirty cops working in the precinct and with what Guy was saying it could very well be true. Could it be that someone was paying them to ignore missing person's cases? If so, that was not good at all. He hated to think that New Orleans was joining the other cities fighting human trafficking.

***

As they sat and ate their dinner, Guy Mayon filled his friend in on the details he had on the case, including information

on the warehouse. He hoped that his gut instincts were
right, and he could trust this man.

Chapter 30

He could taste his blood and the dirt from the floor that his face was being mashed into. Right now, all Josh Comeaux could do was concentrate on breathing.

He grimaced in pain as the goon stepped on his face harder with his heavy boot. He tried not to swallow any of the saliva gathering in his swollen and cut mouth. Instead, he let it trickle out. It left a wet patch on the floor and gathered under his cheek.

He heard the man talking to someone, but Josh couldn't see any other faces. From what it sounded like, it must be a woman. He could also hear the screams coming from his friend. The two of them should have known better than to skip school, but Andy Sinclair convinced Josh he had something cool planned for the day. Josh and Andy had been best friends since Andy moved to Louisiana. His dad was in the Coast Guard, and they transferred here last year. Andy was still upset that he didn't get to stay behind in California and finish high school, so he retaliated as much as possible.

Josh should have known they were headed for trouble when Andy took out the gun he had tucked in the back of his waistband. Josh wished he could start this day over. Just from the look in Andy's eyes, he could tell Andy was up to no good. Josh refused to go into the store when Andy told him that he planned to rob it.

This was New Orleans and the shop owners around here usually kept guns in their store. Neither boy expected to see someone already there collecting money, and that person didn't like when someone else tried to move in on their turf.

At first, Josh thought the gorilla of a man would just scare them, but with the terrifying screams emitting from his friend's mouth, hope died quickly. Josh's dad mentioned before that there were mob connections here in New Orleans. Since Josh watched several mob shows with his dad over the years he knew what they were about to experience would not be pleasant. With each guttural scream, a loud thwack followed.

As Andy's wails weakened, Josh feared that it would soon be his turn. These guys believed in an eye for an eye and a tooth for a tooth, which could only mean they were cutting off Andy's hands since he stole from them, if not worse. Josh shuddered at the idea and feared what they may do to him. Josh should have run as soon as Andy entered the small convenience store, but he stayed behind in case his friend needed him. If only he had gone to school today, none of this would be happening now.

Josh felt himself being lifted up and placed in a chair. The large man just glared down at him and sneered, "Your friend should have known better than to rob one of the businesses we protect. You boosters should know that is against the law here. You, you may get off luckier than your friend." He turned Josh's head towards his friend's dead body. Josh held back the tears threatening to break free and flow down his face.

The man let go of Josh's face and informed him, "The shop owner your friend tried to rob pays for our protection. Y'all picked the wrong time to try your little stunt. These people pay good dough to keep shit like this from happening. Now, what kind of protectors would we be if we can't keep two scrawny kids like you from interfering in our business?"

Before Josh could plead for his life, he saw a woman walking toward him. The way she was dressed had him frozen in fear. Worse, she had a large ass snake dangling from her neck. He was deathly afraid of snakes and almost passed out as she came near him with it.

***

Josh Comeaux's parents paced the living room floor and constantly checked their watches. Bill Comeaux called Andy Sinclair's parents every half hour to see if the boys were there. No one knew where they were, nor had anyone heard from either of them.

The school called Janice Comeaux this morning to let her know that Josh had not shown up for school. She left work immediately to see if he was at home or playing hooky with Andy Sinclair at his house. Neither boy was found at either house.

Ever since Andy came into Josh's life, they had had nothing but problems and now this. She lit a cigarette as she walked around the house with nervous energy. She had a gut feeling that something awful had happened. They called the police, but since Josh was a teenager, they informed her he had to be missing twenty-four hours before they could help. It didn't help that Josh had a record, again thanks to Andy Sinclair.

She doubted the cops would help much due to his recent run-in with the law. They tried calling his cell phone with no luck They even tried tracking it with the cellphone company, but the last location he could be traced to was near Bourbon Street. Then his phone was turned off. She thought about the trouble those two could get into there. What were they thinking of going into that area by themselves?

***

Officers Mark Levine and Joe Mathis were making their nightly patrols when they saw a teenage boy walking down the interstate.

Mathis looked over at his partner, "What do you think this kid is up to?"

As he turned on the lights and sirens, he said, "The kid is probably high as a kite."

They expected the kid to bolt when he heard the sirens, but instead, he kept the same pace, just dragging along. The night was full of motier foux, crazies, but this one took the cake.

As they stepped out of the car, the young man turned around. His appearance stopped them dead in their tracks. Officer Levine yelled out, "Fils de putain! Son of a bitch, Joe what do you think is wrong with this boy?"

He shook his head, "I don't know, but it ain't good; that's for sure."

Mathis looked at the boy, "Quoi ça dit, bougre?"

The young man looked at them and let out an unearthly moan that sent chills down their bodies. They both looked at each other in disbelief and reached for their guns. Levine looked at his partner, "'Etes-vous prêt?"

"Mais oui. Let's go on the count of three."

They rushed the boy at the count of three and took him down with little resistance. This night was one for the record books. Mathis gasped, "I know who this is. I saw the missing person's report on him this morning. His parents reported him missing almost a week ago now. It looks as if he has been on a bender during that time."

Levine looked at his partner, "Mais non, I don't know what is wrong with this boy, but I don't think it has anything to do with drugs. Look at his eyes; they look as if they are lifeless. If I didn't know better, I would say someone stole his soul."

Mathis let out a half disbelieving laugh, "You have been living in this city far too long, mon ami. There is no such thing as voodoo and zombies."

"Mais non? Then how do you explain this. I'm telling you when we get him to the hospital, they will say he's dead."

"Now how are they going to say he's dead when he is walking around? Mais, you have been hanging around these motier foux too long."

Levine shook his head, "Just wait. I'm telling you they will have a hard time finding a heartbeat."

As they walked into the emergency room, Mathis saw Ruth, the night receptionist, "Comment ca va, Ruth?"

She smiled at him, "My night was going fairly well, but if you two are coming in looking all chagrin, then I know my night is going to turn really quick."

Levine chimed in, "We got a live one for you tonight, Ruth."

"Well, bring him on back to room three. We have had a rather quiet hour and I have an open exam room available."

She gasped at the sight of him before asking, "Douce Marie Mère de Dieu. Do either of you know what happened to this poor sha babe?"

Levine scratched his head, "We were kind of hoping the doctor could tell us what was wrong with him. We found him wandering along the interstate just like this."

Ruth took out her stethoscope to listen to the poor boy's heartbeat, but first she looked at Officer Levine and asked, "Mais, you are sure that he is restrained and not going to get me, oui?"

He nodded, "He ain't going to get you Ruth, I promise."

As she went to check his pulse, the young boy let out an unearthly moan. She jumped back, startled, "Mais, they don't pay me enough to deal with this. I will get the doctor."

As she walked out, the two officers looked at each other. Mathis looked down at the boy, "You better behave; you hear me?"

As usual, the boy stared out into space. He hoped the boy's parents arrived soon so they could help deal with him. Maybe they knew what was wrong with him.

Doctor Andrew Thompson walked into the exam room and Mathis let out an inward moan. This doctor would be the one on duty. He was a complete pompous ass, "So officers, what seems to be the problem tonight?"

Mathis explained once again, "We found this boy wandering down the interstate. With you being a doctor and all, we were hoping you could tell us what is wrong with him."

The doctor looked at him with contempt in his eyes. He pulled out his stethoscope and told the young patient, "Son, I need you to take in a deep breath."

As he went to place the stethoscope on the young boy's chest, he lunged at him. Dr. Thompson quickly placed a firm hand on his shoulder and ignored the guttural moans coming from the boy, "Now, I am not in the mood to deal with an uncooperative patient, you hear me? Unlike these two officers here, I have actual work to handle."

The two officers ignored the doctor's snide remarks. They had dealt with him long enough to know to ignore him. As much as they despised his pompous personality, they both knew this doctor may be able to give them some answers as to what was going on with this boy.

They watched as the doctor listened to the teenager's heartbeat. Dr. Thompson looked at the teenager and then his stethoscope. He took his stethoscope and tapped it twice to see if it was working. He placed it on the teen's chest one more time and listened. He looked at the two officers in utter disbelief, "Okay, is this some kind of joke? Did you two gentlemen decide that you had enough of me and wanted to play a sick prank? Let me tell the two of you something; I have patients with serious problems, and I don't need the two of you jerking my chain!"

They both looked at each other. Mathis stated, "Dr. Thompson, this is no joke. We found this boy like this on the interstate. We were hoping you could give us some answers."

He looked at them doubtfully, "If you are pulling some kind of prank, I will have your badges."

Before they could say anything else, the teen's parents barged into the exam room. His mom fainted at the sight. His dad angrily asked, "What the hell is wrong with him?"

Levine responded, "Dr. Thompson is trying to figure that out." He looked over at Dr. Thompson and informed him, "These are the young man's parents. Would you like to explain to the parents what you were just telling us?"

Dr. Thompson glared at the two officers as he bent down to tend to the distraught mother. He reached over to the medicine cabinet and found some smelling salts. It took her a while to come to, "I am sorry for the shock. The nurse should have asked y'all to stay in the waiting room until we were ready for you."

The father explained, "She tried to keep us out there, but we needed to make sure that he is alive. What is wrong with him doctor? Did he overdose or something?"

Dr. Thompson asked the parents, "Does your son have a history of abusing drugs?"

The mother shakily informed him, "No. He swore to us that he didn't do drugs. He said he didn't like the way they made him feel."

"Well, he got a hold of something that is making his body respond abnormally. I will run a tox screen on him to find out what is in his system."

The dad nodded in agreement, "Of course. Do whatever you believe is necessary." The father looked over at the officers, "Why is my son under arrest?"

Mathis replied, "He was found walking down the interstate. When we tried to question him, he lunged at us. Then when the nurse and doctor attempted to treat him, he lunged at them as well. For now, we need to keep him restrained so that he doesn't hurt himself or others."

The mother tried desperately to control her tears, "He has never been a problem child until making friends with that boy. Did you find Adam Sinclair?"

Levine shook his head, "No, ma'am. The only one on the interstate tonight was your son."

She lowered her head, "At least he is alive. Thank God for that. When can he come home?"

Dr. Thompson shook his head, "Not tonight. We need to find out what your son has in his system and why his body is shutting down."

Both parents grabbed for each other, "Is he dying?"

Dr. Thompson looked at them both, "Right now, I don't have any answers for you. I won't know anything more until I complete the exam and the lab has the results. I plan on having everything run stat. Please be patient with us."

Dr. Thompson called Nurse Sinclair over, "Will you see that these two parents get a cup of coffee and find them some place to wait while we finish the exam on their son. Also, I need you to come and draw blood and run it to the lab. We need to get the results back ASAP."

As she showed the parents out the door, she replied, "Right away, Doctor."

***

Dr. Thompson looked at his new patient one more time before beginning his exam. This might be one for the medical journal. The boy was staring off into space, but his vitals were non-existent. While he waited for the tox screen results, he planned to do some research to see if any similar cases were noted.

Chapter 31

Rose Holden had wanted to visit New Orleans and explore the voodoo shops ever since she learned about Louisiana and its unique history this semester. She wanted to bring her family some trinkets and such so she could explain what she learned. She couldn't wait. Growing up, her mother never wanted to come down to New Orleans, even though it wasn't far from Baton Rouge. Her mother swore that it was a different world here, one that she didn't care to know. Rose, on the other hand, found the whole history of the state fascinating, especially New Orleans's history. Now, as she continued to find various mementos to show her parents and younger brothers and sisters, she could envision the expressions on their faces. Her brother would be intrigued by everything she brought home, but her parents may need some convincing. After she had brought her goodies to the counter, the display of voodoo dolls caught her attention.

***

Bianca could tell the girl was a tourist by the assortment of items she was buying. She also met the criteria for one of the girls they needed. She'd overheard the Mafia Prince mention to Brian to be on the lookout for a particular girl and this one met the requirements to a "t". She sent the Mafia Prince a quick text to let him know that he may want to send someone to the shop immediately; she had a girl here that would satisfy his customer's needs. While she waited, Bianca would go ahead and prepare her.

While the girl wasn't looking, she quickly prepared the potion. She would convince the girl to come into the back room for a reading so that she could apply the potion. This would give her high marks with him.

She observed the girl one more time; she couldn't be more than twenty years old. She had the most mesmerizing blue eyes. If there were anyone who could fit the Barbie doll description, it would be this girl. Not only did she have the perfect body, but she had that wholesome quality about her that he was looking for. In the background, the wind chimes made out of driftwood swung in erratic circles. Was her grand-mere's spirit here, warning her against what she had planned?

She ignored the warning and told the alarmed young girl, "Don't worry about that. The air conditioner kicked on, and a breeze is blowing the wind chimes. While you are here, would you like a free reading?"

"Oh, I don't know. I want to make it to Baton Rouge before dark."

Bianca looked at her innocently, "I promise; it won't take long."

As Bianca walked to the back, she called on her magical powers to assist in the potion taking effect faster. She could feel the power course through her body. As she neared the room, a growling resonated throughout the room. Bianca continued to ignore her grand-mere's incessant warning and told the young woman, "Don't worry about that. It is just the old pipes here in the store. Someone is more than likely running the water in one of the other shops."

Nervously, she replied, "Sure."

Suddenly, a thin stream of smoke snaked through the shop startling the young girl enough to cause her to jump. Bianca quickly ushered the young girl into the room and let the heavy velveteen curtains fall that separated the room from the rest of the shop. Inside the room it was somewhat dark, Bianca ushered the girl to the chair while she slipped the potion out of her pocket. As Bianca handed her the tarot cards to shuffle, she poured some of the potion on the cards without her noticing. This was the quickest and easiest way to get the potion absorbed into her skin. She made a mental note to throw away the tarot cards after this so that no one else came into contact with the potion.

As Bianca waited for Brian to come and collect the girl in the back, she prepared another potion for one of her clients. The lady came in asking for something to ward off evil spirits that she believed were haunting her house. Bianca wouldn't doubt the old bat summoned them one night hoping to get them to talk to her. No matter how hard Bianca warned the old woman, she was always trying to get the ghosts that lived in her home to contact her. Bianca warned her time and time again that it could be dangerous to get the spirits to talk to her. Once they have contacted you, it was almost impossible to get them to leave you alone.

The other day she came in asking about a banishing spell, but Bianca gave her a potion to try first to see if that helped. She just needed to place it in various locations to rid them from the house. If this didn't work, then Bianca would offer her services to perform the banishing spell. She would hate to see the old woman try it and do something wrong. That may just anger the spirits even more.

As the door opened, Bianca was adding flower petals and grave dust to the spell to finish it. Brian and a new man he was training stepped into her shop, bringing in the sweltering New Orleans heat. As Bianca made her way around the counter, the bangles around her wrist jangled. She'd hoped she'd see the Mafia Prince as well, but he must have chosen not to come and let Brian handle this on his own. Trying to hide her annoyance, she tucked a strand of hair behind her ear.

She informed them, "She is in the back. I have already given her the potion; she should be controllable now."

Brian asked, "You are sure she is what he is looking for?"

"Very sure. If he doesn't like her, someone else will."

Brian stepped into the back room and nodded his approval, "You are right. She is just what he described." Without thinking, he asked, "So do you think he really has a customer looking for someone like her or do you think she is for him?"

Bianca kept down the jealousy and anger that quickly rose in her, "No, it has to be for a customer. I don't see him wanting someone like her."

"You may be right. I will inform him once we are on our way to see where we should deliver her."

Chapter 32

Alexis was busy shopping along the Riverfront when the aromatic smell of coffee and beignets caught her attention. She stopped at Café Orleans for a café au lait before heading back home. While standing in line, she watched those around her. Despite the stifling heat, the coffee shop was still extremely busy. From where she was standing, she caught sight of an older gentleman playing his saxophone on the corner. She loved coming down here to sit and listen to the jazz players. The man played as if he was actually playing to a particular person. She could feel the love reverberate from the music. She wished she could play music the way he did, but she couldn't carry a tune to save her life.

Something about the man held her fascination. She wasn't sure if it was the way his salt and pepper hair contrasted sharply to his dark caramel colored skin or the fact that despite the oppressive temperature of the day the man wore a black pinstriped suit, crisp white shirt, and a scarlet red bow tie. She noticed that the whole time the man played the tune, he kept his eyes closed, not caring if anyone was around him or not. He continued to pelt away at the music and poured his heart into the song. Several people dropped cash in the saxophone case he left open just for that purpose.

As she dropped a couple of dollars into the growing pile, she wondered just how much money he brought in on a busy day like today. She almost jumped when he replied, "Thank you so much, ma'am." She smiled at him while chastising herself for being so jumpy.

The air was heavy and moist with humidity. It would more than likely storm tonight. She loved listening to the rain at night and the thunder helped to drown out the ghostly sounds that seemed to reverberate through the house. Dominic told her it was just her vivid imagination, but she thought the man could honestly sleep through an earthquake. She, however, swore she had heard drums in her sleep, which was ridiculous. Why would a ghost want to play such a haunting tune on drums? The energy around the plantation had changed. She couldn't quite put her finger on it, but it was as if something evil lurked about. Maybe Dominic was right; she was letting her imagination work overtime. Perhaps she spent too much time on Bourbon Street, in particular the voodoo shops. She had yet to tell Dominic of her frequent visits to the voodoo shops. He would probably laugh at her if she told him that she had her palm read once a week. She doubted he believed in any of the folklores that made up New Orleans.

After purchasing her café au lait, she made her way back to her car. The sidewalks were jam packed with people even though it was the summer. The crowd was a mixture of residents and tourists, the two being easily discernible. Usually, the heat down here deterred them, but they seemed to pay no mind to the rising temperatures today. The aromas coming from the nearby restaurants filled the air, making her mouth water. Maybe it was the good food that brought them here. If she didn't have plans with Dominic tonight, she would stop and pick her up a shrimp po'boy for supper. It would be well worth the extra time she had to spend on the treadmill.

As Alexis walked past Bianca Honore's voodoo shop, a voodoo doll caught her eye. It looked almost exactly like the one in her dream the other night. She found herself drawn into the shop.

The sounds of the drum music in the background were eerily familiar to the ones haunting her dreams. Maybe she had come into the shop too much and it was invading her sleep at night. Until now, she never noticed just how busy Bianca was. The store was packed with people buying various potions and charms.

She couldn't believe how easily people bought into the religion. She walked over to the area where the voodoo dolls were displayed and picked up the voodoo doll from her dreams. She heard Bianca approach, "Cher, did you want a reading today?"

Alexis shook her head, "No, this voodoo doll caught my eye. You won't believe this, but I have been dreaming of a doll almost exactly like this one lately."

"Voodoo dolls can be very powerful if you believe in them. Do you think maybe someone has one of you?"

Alexis put the doll down and shook her head, "Mais non, I think I have been spending too much time in this shop and it is causing me to see the doll in my dreams. Even the music you play in here haunts my dreams."

***

Bianca looked at Alexis with veiled eyes. Dominic must not be giving her enough sleeping potion at night. She must tell him to increase the amount of belladonna. They couldn't have her wake up and notice Dominic not in bed with her. Mais, that wouldn't be good at all. She already didn't get to see her Dominic as much as she would like.

Bianca told Alexis, "That could be. If you want to skip a few readings I understand."

Bianca smiled to herself. She had prepared a voodoo doll very similar to this one to use on Alexis when she married Dominic. Her plan was coming to fruition, but she needed to make sure the woman slept through the night. Bianca's plans were working perfectly for now.

***

As Alexis made her way out of the French Quarter, she saw the hotel where she parked her car. Dominic recently surprised her with a Cadillac CTS-V, burgundy in color. The tan leather interior was soft as a baby's skin and the seats seemed to envelop her. The man knew her so well and knew exactly what she liked. He never even asked her if she wanted a new car; he just drove up in it one day. Her excitement for the gift left her speechless.

The cafes and businesses here were just as busy as the French Quarter. The local businesses must be glad that things were finally picking up after Katrina. This area was lucky, several businesses were left untouched by the destruction Hurricane Katrina left in its wake. Unfortunately, others were demolished and their owners forced to rebuild. It amazed her that despite being scarred by the flood waters, there was still a vibrancy about the city. It just proved that the people here were resilient and there was no holding them down. The residents still had smiles on their faces regardless of the fact that they must rebuild everything they had.

As she neared the hotel, she saw Guy Mayon, the private investigator that stopped by the house a while back. She groaned as he headed towards her.

"Mrs. St. Germaine, will you please look at the missing girl's picture one more time?"

She noticed a stack of flyers that he must be handing out along the Riverfront. "As I told you before, I wouldn't know if she was in any of my husband's establishments or if she worked for him. Dominic keeps his business out of the home and I have never had any interest in what he does to be honest with you."

"Please, maybe you have seen her in passing around New Orleans."

Alexis looked at the flyer one more time. She felt sorry for the family and what they must be going through. The young girl was barely twenty years old and last seen in New Orleans six weeks ago. She looked so carefree in the picture. Alexis wondered if she ran away from home. "Is there a chance that she just doesn't want to be found?"

"I don't think so. She went to college here in New Orleans and checked in with her parents who live in Baton Rouge at least once a week. She goes home on Sundays for lunch and to do her laundry. Her mom sends her back with all kinds of food and goodies to tide her over for the week."

"I take it the parents hired you to find her."

He looked at her intently, "I specialize in missing persons. Her parents felt they were getting the brush off from the local police force here and asked if I could help them out."

Alexis shook her head, "You know there is a chance that she just wants some time to herself and took off for a bit."

She watched as he pursed his mouth, "Is this coming from personal experience?"

Her mouth went dry as his gaze bore right into her, "Let's just say that sometimes parents ask more from us than we are ready to actually give."

"So, I take it your parents expected a lot out of you?"

She gave him a shaky grin, "They had their expectations. Look, I'm sorry about the missing girl, but I haven't seen her. I really do wish I could help."

"If you see her or hear anything, please give me a call."

"Do you have a gut feeling on this girl?"

He nodded, "I don't think she ran away. From what I have learned about her, she was very dedicated to her studies and her grades were good. I think she ran into some trouble and from what I learned about her, she isn't very street smart."

A chill ran down Alexis's spine. There were evil people out there who preyed on the innocent. "Do you at least have any leads?"

"She was last seen buying a voodoo doll for her mother as a birthday gift. She stopped at a little shop on Bourbon Street to buy her an authentic one, but after that her trail grows cold."

Alexis could only imagine who the poor girl may have run into on Bourbon Street on a Saturday. The streets were crawling with tourists and locals on most days, but the weekends and nights were the busiest times there.

New Orleans was busy this afternoon; everyone wanted to enjoy this beautiful weather. Pedestrians strolled along the sidewalk, mostly window shopping and cars drove by in a hurry to get to their destination. As Alexis walked back to her car, she noticed for the first time all the flyers for missing girls and even children, that were plastered all over the city. How had she not seen these before? She shuddered at what these families were going through, the uncertainty. Their lives suspended in a distressing limbo. A breeze blew off of the river breaking her out of her reverie.

By the time Alexis made it home, she was completely unnerved by the day's happenings. She couldn't help but think about those poor missing women. Her visit to Bianca's shop and seeing the voodoo doll that haunted her dreams also had her a little anxious. She just couldn't explain it. By the time Dominic made it home that night, she simply wanted to forget about the day's happenings.

She ran into his arms and kissed him passionately. She whispered in his ear, "Let's skip our plans. Make love to me."

He needed no further prompting. He swept her up into his arms and carried her off to the bedroom.

Chapter 33

When the Mafia Prince saw the warehouse from the Mississippi River, he automatically knew that it was exactly what he had been looking for. The location was perfect. They could either load the women up straight onto a boat or right from the warehouse. The windows were set up high and barely big enough for anyone to slip through. You would have to climb the wall to get in or out of this place by the windows.

He would black out the windows so that no one noticed the lights were on in the place. To the outside world, the old warehouse would appear abandoned and unless they did some digging, they would never know it belonged to his family. Hell, when he found it, he was surprised to learn that his family already owned the building. It had remained empty and unused for quite some time now. He wondered what the old warehouse may have been used for.

His driver eased the car over the bumpy road trying to avoid at least the deeper potholes that plagued the old road leading to the warehouse. He considered having the road repaired, but then there was a chance that people would start to wonder why repairs were being done. He didn't want attention drawn to the warehouse with what he had planned for it. As they got closer, he lowered his window and breathed in the night air. He wanted to listen for any noises that may be heard around here. From what he had seen, the entire area seemed to be abandoned, but he needed to make sure that their activities would go unnoticed.

When he stepped into the warehouse, it was bigger than he initially thought. Not only was the place large enough to hold all the women, but they could have the auction right here. His customers could pull their cars into the warehouse and stay hidden from anyone that may notice cars gathering around the warehouse. There was also a nice sized office and a makeshift bathroom. It may not have all the comforts of home, but at least, he could have someone stay here and guard the place. There was an area upstairs where they could hold the women and the downstairs area could be used for the ones they wished to auction. A loading dock in the rear of the warehouse led right to the river, so if needed, they could load the girls right onto a boat and out to the Gulf of Mexico. Arrangements were being made already for some of the girls to be brought to China and sold from there. He was also making arrangements for other international selling spots as well.

He looked down at his watch and grimaced. Lately, he had been working some very late nights, and his wife was beginning to complain. She had also been asking a lot of questions, questions that he didn't want to answer. He didn't share the details of his business with her, no matter how much she asked.

Hell, he didn't even talk to his business associates about his socialite wife. Besides, they wouldn't be interested in hearing how she dragged him to the ballet and charity functions. He kept his private life just that, private. He didn't want any of them to use his personal life against him. He had been careful to make sure that he had no bridges between the two and planned to keep it that way.

Chapter 34

The club filled up quickly as work let out and men poured in wanting to relax after a hard week at work. Friday night was one of their busiest nights, especially on paydays – which happened to be today. This strip club may be seedy by New Orleans standards, but since they kept the prices low, patrons continued to come back.

The house rules for the bartender were the first drink came from a barely watered down bottle of alcohol; as the customer continued ordering drinks, the drinks became watered down more. This kept costs down and it helped with the number of belligerent drunks in the strip club. The men were drunk enough to spend money and not realize that the alcohol was watered down. However, they were not drunk enough to cause trouble. If they did cause trouble, there were several large bouncers strategically roaming around the room that resolved any problems.

Brian Donovan observed a group of young men sauntering into the club. He doubted they were barely legal to enter, but the way they dressed screamed yuppies. He nodded his head to the bouncer to allow them to stay. These boys would likely spend a wad of dough and were probably looking to get laid. One of the girls here would be more than willing to comply.

Currently, he was waiting impatiently as the stripper counted out her dough in the palm of his hand. Brian suspected that she was holding out on the Family, and that was never good.

She stuttered, "I don't have it all for you, but I promise I am good for it." She looked at him slyly and grabbed at him,

"Unless you can think of another way I can work off what I owe you."

He slapped her hand away and looked at her in disgust, "Babe, I don't want what you have to offer. The Boss isn't going to like that you don't have his dough."

She took a step back, "I promise I will get it to you tomorrow."

He grabbed her by the throat and informed her, "I will be back tomorrow to collect."

Taking a good look at her, she was perfect for a recent request. They had a client looking for a young woman just like her. He would do as he said and give her until tomorrow to pay, but then he would make sure she understood the importance of paying. She would bring in more than she owed.

Before leaving, he asked around about her. He was pleased to learn that she had no family to miss her if she did disappear. *Yes, she was perfect for the client after all.*

***

The stench of cheap alcohol and urine permeated Bourbon Street in these early morning hours. Soon, this area would be crawling with people busy making deliveries, which would later be consumed by the hordes of tourists that flooded the French Quarter.

As Sherrie Wilson walked past a bar that stayed open twenty-four hours a day, she caught a whiff of the stale smoke and beer that floated out the open doors. Music and the sound of slurred voices drifted outside. She resisted the urge to join in the fun. Most of the patrons in this bar, unlike the club she worked in, were tourists looking to have a good time and to share stories about their visit to New Orleans. At one time, she was one of those tourists until the city lured her in with its temptations. She stopped to peer into the bar and observed the fun before moving on. She wondered how many of these tourists would be arrested before the day was out, or maybe something much worse would happen to them. There were deep, dark secrets that lurked about in this area. She had her own dark secrets that she wanted to keep hidden as well; maybe that was why she loved this place.

She was running from a past that she feared would catch up to her. Had her parents even missed her? She had been on the move ever since she ran away from home, afraid that they would find her and bring her home. This was the first place that she had stayed for any length of time. She felt as if she belonged here, but lately she feared that something was closing in on her. Maybe it was time to move on. She didn't want to be found and she definitely didn't want to go home.

The drugs and alcohol helped her to forget her past to some degree. She wished she could go back and change time. Maybe if she had been brave enough to tell her parents what happened, they could have helped her. But he'd warned her that if she spoke one word about what happened to anyone, he would kill those she loved. He placed the blame on her, saying that she used her body to tease him, always giggling when he was near and vying for his attention. She loved him like an uncle, until that fateful night. That night she lost her virginity to her dad's best friend. She thought he loved her like a daughter, but that was not what he intended. Was he right? Was it her fault?

After what he did to her, she could not look her parents in the eyes; she was so ashamed.

As she left the bar, she overheard a conversation between two tourists who were moving on to another bar, "Man this place is great. Bars everywhere and everything is open twenty-four hours a day."

The friend slapped his other friend on the shoulder and laughed, "Tell me about it. Only down here can you find drive thru daiquiri shops."

As Sherrie made the turn to the hotel, she popped another ecstasy. This was how she found the inner strength to perform the acts required of her. She owed a lot of money to men that she should have never become involved with. If she wanted to stay alive, she needed to do as she was told.

As the drug took effect, she started to feel strange. With unsteady steps, she became more disoriented. From where she was located, she should be able to see the Mississippi River and the riverboats docked along the pier. Instead, the glittering lights danced in the night sky, and she was unsure where her landmarks were. Live jazz music filled the night air. This city never seemed to sleep, and the southern nights here were just as seductive as a lover's kiss.

She wasn't sure if it was the drugs affecting her this way, but her surroundings took on a magical glow. She forced herself to push forward, but her legs grew heavier with every step.

As she tried to make her way to the hotel, she stumbled into the shadows of the alley. She leaned back against a wall trying to gather her senses before entering the hotel. The drugs she took must have been more potent that she realized. She couldn't stay here long. This was where the gutter bums and street workers liked to hang out. Those that lived in New Orleans knew to avoid the alleys in this area, especially at night.

A movement behind her caught her attention. She pushed herself off of the wall and decided to leave. She never saw the dark figure move in behind her. She never had a chance to scream.

Chapter 35

Graham Stevenson wasn't sure what he was addicted to the most, but when you added all of his vices together, it equaled trouble. They had been filming in New Orleans, Louisiana for about six weeks and in that time, he became indebted to some dangerous people.

He looked at the bottle of scotch and cocaine he had received earlier today. Of course, it came with a stern warning; if he wanted to keep his pretty face, he would pay up by the end of the day.

Graham drained his bank account the other day in hopes of a winning streak at the poker game. Instead, he found himself even deeper in debt to these people. The man that came to collect the debt said he understood and gave him until the end of the week. When he came to Graham's hotel room Friday night, he wasn't as understanding when he discovered Graham still did not have the money. Graham worried that he would do something to his face or body which would leave him with a lot of explaining to do to the director the next morning. After listening to Graham's pleading, the man concurred that it was in no one's best interest if Graham couldn't act the next day. So the man was "nice" enough to merely dislocate his arm. Graham had never felt such an intense pain in all of his life. After explaining that a stunt had gone wrong, the emergency room doctor had set it. It still hurt and was a constant reminder that he owed a large amount of money. When he walked into his trailer during a break and saw the scotch and cocaine, he thought his luck had changed until he saw the note attached; payment would be collected tonight or else.

He picked up the scotch and poured himself a tumbler full. Not bothering with the ice, he downed the drink in one swallow. The fiery drink sent a warmth throughout his body. He eyed the cocaine and decided if this was his last night on this earth he may as well enjoy himself. As he snorted the drug into one nostril, he looked at the other line longingly. One hit did not satisfy the need he had. He needed more. As he was about to snort the other line, he heard someone knocking on the hotel room door. Wiping his nose, he walked over and peered through the small hole to see who was there, unsure if he wanted to know.

He was taken aback by the gorgeous young girl. Clearly she must have the wrong room. He didn't ask for companionship tonight.

He cracked open the door, "You must have the wrong room. Sorry."

She placed her small foot in the door opening, "I don't think I do. I was sent to collect some money you owe."

Graham opened the door and peered around to see if this was a set up. Not seeing anyone else, he quickly ushered her into his room. He asked the young girl, "Exactly why did they send such a beautiful woman, instead of someone from the goon squad?"

She smiled slyly at him, "He is hoping I can convince you to pay up without someone damaging that pretty face of yours."

Graham returned her smile. If this was how the Mafia Prince collected his debts, maybe the man couldn't be so bad. He didn't see how this woman could hurt him. What she wore left little to the imagination, and he didn't see where she could possibly carry a gun. This woman standing before him was the perfect package. Her velvety skin reminded him of a luscious dark honey. "Honey, you are the best debt collector that I have ever seen, but I don't have his money."

She walked over to him and pushed him towards the bed, "Well then I will need to show you the importance of paying won't I?"

He pulled her closer to him, "And just what do you have in mind?"

Her eyes seemed to see right through to his soul. They were the most intriguing green. There was clearly an infusion of Caucasian and Creole blood in her family. "I was told that I can screw your brains out? Will that be okay with you?"

He bet she would be a good lay. Before the night was over, he planned to do all kinds of degrading things to this one. There were quite a few things that he wanted to try and since she had come to his room willingly, he doubted she would go to the authorities.

The lean muscles in her body rippled in perfect symmetry as she straddled him. Her brown skin glistened in the soft light of the room. His imagination began to stir at all the things she could do to him. He couldn't wait to see what it would be like to have this young thing ride him. She was sure to be one hell of a wild ride. From somewhere on that luscious little body of hers, she pulled out a small cat o nine tails whip. He immediately became aroused. It looked as if she may be into the same little games as him. This night was looking up.

She ordered him, "Lay back. I'm going to tie you up."

He was quick to do as she said, anxious to play this little game. He had been hoping to restrain her, but this was just as exciting. After both of his arms had been restrained to the headboard, she took the whip and lashed at him rather forcibly. He winced at the sharp pain. She told him, "You know you borrowed money from the wrong people don't you?"

His quick temper flared immediately. This was not the game he had in mind. He tried to break free from the restraints, but they were too tight. "I told the other guy that I would have the money and I will."

She leaned down and kissed him hard on the lips before whipping him again. This time the whip struck him across the balls and the pain was instantly searing. "You have a smart mouth don't you. You need to do a better job keeping it under control."

He tried to control his anger, "Look, I swear that I will get his money to him as soon as I can." This night wasn't going as he expected at all. Now, he was unsure of exactly what this woman planned for him and with his arms restrained he could not fight her off.

When he went to speak again, he couldn't find his voice. The cocaine must have been stronger than he thought. The room swayed as nausea started deep inside of him. He feared he would be sick all over himself if he didn't get up. He forced the words out, "Please, I don't feel well. I think I am going to be sick. You need to release me so I can go to the bathroom."

She just laughed down at him and stepped off the bed with ease. As she walked away from the bed, the contents of his stomach expelled all over himself and the bed.

A fiery pain gripped his stomach. He tried to find a comfortable position on the bed as the bitch stood there and laughed at him. The pain in his gut suddenly radiated to his crotch.

The woman before him seemed to change before his eyes. She stared down at him with a demonic evil in her eyes. Even though his body was weak, he tried to free himself from the restraints once again.

He asked, "What... What did you do to me?"

She gave him a maniacal laugh, "Mais, what did I do to you? I haven't touched you now have I?"

He tried to curl up in a fetal position, "Please, you have to help me."

She looked into his eyes and could see the sheer terror there. "The less you fight it, the less the pain will be."

He could only take quick pants as the pain seared his body. How did she do this to him? Did someone poison the booze or maybe the drugs? Was this how he would pay his debt back to The Mafia Prince, through death? Was the woman here to make sure he died in agony? He begged her one more time, "Please make the pain stop."

He begged God to spare him. He would change his ways; he promised. He would be a better person and more generous with his money. He would stop sinning as much if only he were given a chance to live.

He gasped aloud as another jolt of pain hit him. As the sheer agony took over his body, his world was sent into total blindness.

Someone whispered in his ear, "You will find no peace. You will be among the walking dead."

"Please, I don't want to die." It was getting harder to breath. The bitter taste of vomit remained thick in his mouth.

She watched what happened to his body as he stopped fighting. His eyes fluttered before he finally welcomed the darkness.

***

The maid knocked on the door and waited for an answer. Not hearing a response, she used her master key to enter the room. After calling out and receiving no response, she stepped into the room.

She was frozen in place at the sight in front of her. She was horrified at what she saw and called out to him, "Mister, mister, are you okay?"

Not receiving any response, she walked over to see if he was alive. She quickly made the sign of the cross and backed out of the hotel room. She learned a long time ago not to scream when you found a body; it just brought everyone rushing into the room. Instead, she locked the door and went to find the manager.

***

Detective Mike Bailey looked down at the body and wondered who this man crossed paths with last night. The dead man's eyes stared up at the ceiling, devoid of any life. His skin had an ashen look about it. The smell of death hung heavy in the air.

Dried vomit clung to the man's face as well as the bed and floor. Looking at the cocaine on the nightstand and the bottle of scotch, this was more than likely an overdose But he couldn't make that call; it had to be done by the coroner.

Detective Bailey instructed the crime scene techs, "Just in case the coroner comes back with a homicide ruling, take as many pictures of the crime scene as you can please. Once we release the scene, housekeeping will come in here and remove any evidence that may be left behind."

The young officer responded, "Yes, sir, but you do know this place is a cesspool for fingerprints and the like."

"Yeah, I know, but try to do the best you can." Detective Bailey hoped that it was ruled an overdose so he could close this file.

Chapter 36

Guy Mayon walked into the strip club with one thing on his mind and it didn't have anything to do with the services these girls offered. From what he'd ascertained so far, a few of the missing girls worked here when they disappeared. Could this be one of the ways they found the perfect girls to use for their sex slave ring?

The strip club was the perfect front since it was easier to find out who would not be missed. These girls were liable to talk to one another in the dressing room; they probably shared with each other their problems, boyfriends and family history. Once the traffickers knew for sure which girls wouldn't be missed, they acted. This time the estranged daughter thought that her family didn't care about her, but she was wrong. They missed her terribly and desperately wanted their daughter back.

Hopefully, by visiting the strip club in the afternoon the girls would talk to him. The place would be full by nighttime, and they wouldn't be able to answer any questions. He planned on management noticing him as well. He wanted to rattle someone to the point of talking because so far no one was breathing a word about any of the missing girls.

As he entered the dim bar, the smoke seemed to envelop him. The club was busier than he thought it would be at this time. There were ten guys at the stage and five more at the bar. As he found an empty seat at the stage, the young woman dancing appeared bored out of her mind. The girl was skin and bones; he wondered when she last ate. By the redness of her nose, the only thing she cared about was her nose candy and not food. At one time, she was probably an attractive woman, but now the drugs were destroying her body. Her auburn hair had an oily sheen to it and fell limp against her shoulders. The tattoos covering her body more than likely were to help hide her track marks. Her pasties looked as if they were put on in haste, as if she was just shoved on stage. Her g string looked two sizes too big and kept slipping. She was so dazed that he doubted she even cared.

Guy pulled out a five and waved it to the cocktail waitress. It amazed him how the cocktail waitresses always appeared to be hotter than the dancers. She dressed just as scantily as the dancer. To this day, he hadn't figured out the idea behind the pasties and g strings. It wasn't like they hid anything, but someone decided years ago that the girls should attempt to cover their private parts. It made no sense to him, but then again, most of the rules and regulations in this world made no sense. That was one of the reasons he left the force. He was enforcing laws that made absolutely no sense and worse, some of his coworkers felt since they were the ones in power, they didn't need to abide by the same rules as others.

When she came over he told her, "Give me a coke please."

She looked at him, "Anything in it?"

"Nope, just soda."

She walked off in a huff, realizing he wouldn't be one of her normal customers that got drunk and forgot about the change she owed them. When she came back, he handed her a twenty. "Can you sit down for a moment? I have a few questions about a girl that used to work here."

She looked around nervously, "You aren't a cop or something are you?"

"No, nothing like that. Her family asked that I look for her. Her name is Sherrie Wilson. I promise I won't take a lot of your time."

She still needed convincing that he was not a cop, so she said, "Sherrie said that she didn't have a family."

He took out the picture of her and her family that her parents gave him. It was from a few years before she disappeared, "Here she is with her parents and her brother. They miss her very much."

"I don't think she wants to be found. She said that she and her parents don't see eye to eye on some major things."

He told her, "They realize they may have been too hard on her. She is their only daughter, and they didn't like the crowd she ran with back then. They never thought she would run away and not contact them. They want to make amends. They don't care what she has done; they just want her back home."

"I wish I could help, but Sherrie just never showed up for work one day. We assumed she was ready to move on. She told us one night how she gets tired of staying in one place for too long and she would hitch a ride to another city to start over."

He looked her in the eyes, "So you honestly think she just decided to move on."

"It's not unheard of here. It's not like this is a job worth having or anything. It gets the bills paid," she looked over to the dancer, "or pays for your drugs."

Guy considered the possibility that the girl just left the city and went somewhere else. It fit her time frame. She only stayed in one place for a few months at a time, never more than a year. His gut told him differently this time. He suspected that she didn't leave the city willingly this time, but as with the others, he had no proof that they were part of the sex slave ring. If only he had a clue where they could be holding these girls or who was involved in the trafficking ring. If he found a low man on the totem pole, he may be able to convince that person to help out.

After the cocktail waitress had left, he turned his attention to the stage. He wondered if the young woman was too drugged to talk to him; he doubted she could form a sentence right now.

Once the music stopped, the woman clomped off of the stage, and the DJ announced that Amber was coming up. The guys around him continued to nurse their drinks. He watched in dismay as the next young woman had the same dazed look as the previous girl. She just stared out into space as she danced. As he stood, he couldn't help but notice her eyes. Something about them was eerie to say the least. He saw her dancing, but there was no life in her eyes. He shrugged his shoulders; working in a place like this probably sucked the life right out of you.

***

Congressman Randy Sanders looked at his newest purchase with wanton desire. From what he'd seen so far, she was well worth the exorbitant amount of money he paid for her. Unfortunately, he wouldn't know how good she was until they arrived at their destination. Until then, he raised the privacy glass so that he could at least get a feel for what he'd bought.

***

The limo driver watched as the privacy glass went up and shuddered when he looked at the woman in the back seat. He couldn't explain it, but something was not quite right about her.

***

As Congressman Sanders's limo merged onto the interstate from the entrance ramp, the driver didn't see the eighteen wheeler behind him as it lost control. The eighteen wheeler hit an oil slick on the interstate and the massive vehicle lost traction. He honked his horn as a warning, but it was too late for anyone in his path.

The truck driver clutched his steering wheel and pounded on the brakes in an attempt to lessen the effects of the impending accident. He felt his trailer slide to the left before hitting the limousine entering the interstate. He watched in horror as the limo careened through the air and hit the cement wall before bouncing off and spinning around in circles. He called immediately for help, thankful that the road was almost deserted at this hour.

***

When Detective Mike Bailey and his partner, Detective Stan Gaudet, arrived at the scene, Bailey could tell from the looks on everyone's faces that the outcome wasn't good. The accident involved a hooker and one of the congressmen. This would be a long night. He asked the responding officer, "Why were we called to the accident?"

"Well, sir, the hooker is one of the women your friend was asking about. I thought you might like to know."

He walked over to the ambulance where First Responder Hebert was working on the girl, "I am sorry sir. I thought for a moment she had a pulse, but if there was a faint one it is gone. The Congressman died on impact."

Detective Bailey looked at the young girl and hated that he had to call Guy Mayon, but at least he would be able to bring the family some closure.

Chapter 37

Brian walked into his Boss's office; unsure of why he was summoned. Usually, when his Boss had a job, he just sent him the instructions, but this time, he was told to come in.

"Brian, I have a job for you and I don't want you to collect dough. It isn't a job for the cleaner either. I want this man brought in alive for a special project. Can you do that?"

"Of course, Boss."

Brian cringed as a slow smile formed across his Boss's face, "I have something special planned for this man. I need him alive for questioning, and once we have what we want, he will be tended to. Bianca has special plans for him, and I want her to be able to carry them out."

"No problem."

His Boss warned him, "Just be careful; this guy is good at avoiding us but no more. It is time he pays up. When you capture him, he is liable to kill himself just to avoid what is to come."

***

Everything seemed to happen in fast motion. He told himself that he should drop to the ground and accept the unavoidable - his death was near.

He heard the gun fire and felt the bullet enter his body. He stumbled backwards from the impact. The blood slowly colored his shirt in a flower like pattern.

The bullet made a cruel path through his body, shattering bone as it exited. He waited for the pain that was sure to follow such an invasion to his body. As he fell to the ground, a coldness washed over him. He tried to draw a breath, but he could barely gasp as darkness invaded his world. In under a minute, his life came to an end. His blood spilled from his body and covered the ground.

If only he could call out and beg for someone to help him. He felt his body being lifted and wondered if someone was here to help him. Blood shot from his mouth as he gurgled and gasped. He felt his body being thrown into the air. Water washed over him.

His forty years of life had come to this. No one would ever know what happened to him. As his body sank to the bottom of the mighty Mississippi River, he slipped into eternal darkness.

***

Brian Donovan looked down at the body of his latest hit and shook his head. He'd worked as an enforcer for The Family almost five years now, collecting debts owed as well as other jobs. One day he hoped to make rank as a cleaner. The cleaner's only job was to take out people ordered by their Boss. Brian still had been unable to figure out who was the current cleaner.

This whole mess could have been prevented, but instead, the babbo (idiot) had to run. As he hoisted the body over his shoulder, he noticed how eerie the victim's blood looked on the sidewalk. He had to hide the large spot to keep it from being noticed. Not too far away, he spotted a bag of trash. He drug it over to hide the spot for now. He kept a few bottles of bleach in his trunk for circumstances just like this. If all went well, he should have time to cover his tracks before anyone woke up.

On his way back to his car, Brian pulled out a cigarette and surveyed the area. He made sure that there weren't any witnesses lurking about. The Mafia Prince had half the police force working for him, but Brian didn't want to take any chances.

As Brian dropped the body into the car, he jumped when the body twitched. He chuckled when he realized it was just a response from the dead man's nervous system. Brian snuffed out his cigarette and flicked it on to the dead man. No sense in leaving behind any trace evidence, one could never be too careful nowadays.

He pulled out a bottle of bleach and made his way back to the murder scene. He hid in the shadows to keep from being noticed.

Next he had to dispose of the body. There was a bend in the river where the current would take the victim far from here. He tossed Andrew Hauffman into the water, and watched as the body sank into the murky water of the Mississippi River. He had killed numerous people, and it never ceased to amaze him how one minute you were here and the next minute you ceased to exist.

The Mafia Prince had given Brian specific instructions to bring Andrew Hauffman in for the voodoo woman to perform black magic on him. Brian did not expect Andrew to run; he had no choice but to fire the gun. Thankfully, the gun was equipped with a silencer so no one heard a gunshot, although he doubted anyone would even blink at the sound of a gunshot around here. Crime in New Orleans was back to an all time high.

Brian sure hoped that his Boss wasn't too upset about the fact that he shot Andrew Hauffman. The man was a joke and a wimp for even running from his fate. He should have expected this would happen to him. You don't borrow dough from the Mafia Price and expect not to pay it back. He was informed of the rules regarding repayment before entering into this business relationship just like everyone else.

Chapter 38

Bianca watched as her first group of zombies returned to the cabin. Now that her power was stronger, she sent out their zombies into the night to steal and cause trouble for some of their enemies. When the cops heard the victims' complaints, they just looked at them like they were crazy. Who would believe that a zombie robbed them? Plus, these zombies weren't like those in the movies. She instructed them as to what they were supposed to do and they didn't just wander around looking for brains to eat. She was careful to feed them only animals and those that the Mafia Prince needed to dispose of.

The zombies made the perfect slaves. During the day, they worked in the fields or sweat shops preparing merchandise that the Family sold. At night, they pillaged where they were sent. Bianca was careful where she sent them as to not alarm anyone who stumbled upon her creations.

Regarding the captured girls, she had no problems with what her Boss did with the girls technically, but she had seen what evil lurked behind some of these men's eyes. With the money the men paid it would do no good to have a woman unwilling to submit to their wishes. She cast a spell on the women that enabled them to endure the pain that was forced on them by their owner.

Now that her power was strengthening, she could perform the more difficult voodoo spells. The one spell she found most helpful was the transposing spell. She was able to move back and forth between various places without ever worrying about time. At first when she would perform the spell, it weakened her significantly, but now she could move at ease several times during the day with no side effects.

She wondered if her Mafia Prince knew just how strong she was becoming. He warned those around him not to cross him, but she was the one they should be worried about and the stronger she became the more they should worry.

As much as she loved her Mafia Prince, she would never give up this power! She doubted anyone could compete with her now. She was almost invincible. Her grand-mere wanted her to become powerful in voodoo; she was getting her wish. Although this was not the kind of magic she wanted her to practice. Her grand-mere had strictly warned her against the practice of black magic. Perhaps that was what drew Bianca to it. Bianca had never liked being told she couldn't do something.

Bianca also felt that her lover was cheating on her. If that were the case, he would rue the day he'd deceived her. She would put a curse on him that he would never forget.

Chapter 39

Brian broke into the drug dealer's house with complete ease. He shook his head at how much of an imbecile this man must be. Not only did the man believe he could short change his Boss, but he also thought he had free access to as much dope as he wanted instead of selling it all and bringing the Boss the dough.

He found the dealer passed out in bed with a beautiful woman. He wondered if the Boss's dough paid for her. With both passed out, more than likely from a heavy dose of free drugs, he quickly restrained them in a chair without either waking up. He went into the kitchen, poured two glasses of ice water and doused each with a cup.

They woke up sputtering. The man let out a string of obscenities that would make even some men blush. The beauty sat there looking dazed and soon tears pooled in her eyes.

Brian looked at the drug dealer, "You owe the Mafia Prince some dough. I want to know where the rest is!"

Instead of answering Brian, the hostage glared at him in frustration and tried to free himself from the restraints. He soon realized it was futile. Brian had the duct tape so tight that it cut off the circulation to his hands.

Brian grabbed the drug dealer's hair, forcing him to look up at him. "I am not going to keep asking you this, where is the dough?"

As Brian held his head back, the man spat in his face. Using his free hand, Brian took his pistol and struck him across the temple. The sharp contact with the gun split open the man's face. Blood trickled down his face as the man glared at him with pure hatred. Brian wasn't going to get anywhere with the man and walked over to the beauty.

He looked at the man and informed him, "I guess since you can take the pain; I need to see how well she likes pain." He took the barrel of the gun and let it glide down her body. She cringed in fear.

The hostage shouted out, "You leave her alone. She has nothing do with this."

Brian looked at him with a sinister smile. Now, he knew how to get this man to talk. Brian would be careful on how he roughed this beauty up though. He would get a nice finder's fee from the Mafia Prince with her, but only if she wasn't covered in bruises. Their customers were the ones that liked to leave the bruises and had no desire to purchase a girl already roughed up.

He looked at the woman, "Tell me where your boyfriend over there keeps the dough?"

She looked over at the drug dealer in fear. Brian knew that the dough or drugs had to be somewhere around here. This man wouldn't be stupid enough to use all of the drugs for himself. He'd received his delivery three days ago. Besides, he watched him make several sales last night and then came here to crash. It had to be here somewhere.

Instead of answering Brian, she just cried more. This frustrated him to no end. Why must women cry all the time?

Out of frustration, he grabbed a hold of the woman's pinky and snapped it back. He heard the bones in her finger break. She howled in pain.

He looked at the drug dealer, "You better tell me where the drugs and dough are stashed, or it will only get worse for your comare."

Without waiting for a response, he took another finger and snapped it easily in two. The fingers could be mended in no time without taking away from her overall beauty. Besides, if Brian didn't come back with something, then he would have some explaining to do. Both hostages remained silent, and he took this as a sign of disrespect for not only him but the Mafia Prince as well.

If he fired his gun, it would draw unwanted attention. He walked over to the drug dealer and took the butt of his gun and slammed it down on the man's balls. With him being tightly restrained, he could merely writhe and howl in pain. This was payback for trying to undermine his authority.

He looked down at the man, "Now, do you want me to do something similar to your girl?"

The man stuttered from the intense pain he suffered from, "Dude that was uncalled for. What I have collected and have left is under the bed. Just check it out."

Brian walked into the bedroom and only counted three hundred dollars and a few baggies of drugs, "This is no where near enough dough. What happened to the rest of the drugs?"

The drug dealer shrugged his shoulders, "I didn't think the Boss would mind if I tried out some of his stuff. That way I can advertise how primo the stuff is."

Brian looked down at the man with complete disdain, "Well, mon ami, that is where you are wrong." In one swift movement, he broke the man's neck. The woman saw the lifeless body of her boyfriend and let out a blood curdling scream. Without thinking, he picked up the butt of the gun and hit the young woman over the top of her head knocking her unconscious. He had to move quickly in case someone called the police after hearing the scream.

He hit the button on his car remote to open the trunk. Rushing, he dumped the unconscious girl in the trunk and left.

As Brian drove to the warehouse, he yawned. He still had the package in the trunk of his car to drop off before heading home. By the time he could crawl into bed and get some much needed sleep, the sun would be coming up. Thankfully, he only had one person who refused to cooperate with him tonight. Even though he did not get all the dough owed to his Boss, he did retrieve something that would bring in more money than what the drug dealer owed the Mafia Prince.

Chapter 40

The Mafia Prince wanted to be at the warehouse before his guests arrived. He wanted to ensure that the girls were ready to be shown. Tonight must go off without a hitch. He had a lot riding on this. If anything went wrong, then this whole thing would be a bust and someone else was sure to move in and take his place. No, he had to make certain that nothing went wrong and he stressed to everyone that worked for him just how important tonight was.

For tonight's show, he'd ordered a makeshift stage in the middle of the room. Until the auction started, the girls were held in cages downstairs. Bianca arrived early this morning to ensure that they were all zombies. He wanted the girls manageable tonight and would not stand for one crying or begging to be set free; mais non that would not do at all. The girls were given a small enough dose where they were controllable, but not unmovable. With each winning bidder, they would be given the word that allowed him complete control over the young girl.

Lights had been arranged around the stage to accentuate the young bodies. He wanted the bidders tempted with lust from the beginning. Each girl was given a good shower beforehand. It would do him no good if they came in here dirty and sweaty; instead, when they walked on the stage, their perfectly made up bodies would glisten when the light hit them. Bianca had developed a body spray that released the girls' pheromones into the crowd as well as making their skin glow. It worked so well, that they were thinking of mass marketing the body spray. Bianca used it herself. She said that it made her skin feel baby soft. Hell, she may have come up with the fountain of youth without knowing it.

The Mafia Prince puffed on his cigar as six of the girls were brought downstairs and arranged in the cages. The girls in this group were teenagers. They were naked except for the voodoo necklaces that Bianca adorned them with and the stiletto heels they each wore. When he looked into their eyes, he saw nothingness. The drug worked perfectly; although, he personally liked to see some life in the eyes of the woman he was about to screw.

It never ceased to amaze him how well this zombie drug worked at controlling these girls. Tonight would be the largest auction he had ever done. Tonight's auction would include over one hundred girls and women of various ages which was why he wanted to make sure they were controllable. Too much could go wrong; this business could be unpredictable when you were holding someone against their will.

Typically, they sold the girls outright, but when he discovered they did this in other parts of the world, he wanted to try it here as well. Mais, he wanted to corner the market on this and bring more people to his lovely city. The more people that came to New Orleans, the more money he made all around. What with the hotels, casinos, car dealerships and so on all of his businesses would grow.

Human trafficking was becoming a fast growing business and it was about time that this family had joined in the ranks. Human trafficking was now among the top three of the largest criminal activities. Drug trafficking and arms smuggling were still the top two illegal activities, but the Mafia Prince felt as if they may strike gold with this human trafficking bit. It was becoming more difficult to move the drugs, but the women should be easier, especially if he kept them permanently in a zombie state.

He knew to stay ahead of his competition; he needed the best looking girls. Lucky for him, this city and the surrounding areas were teeming with a broad assortment of beautiful young girls. The selection was inexhaustible. Mardi Gras was the best time for them to stock up on women. The streets were crowded with inebriated girls, and if they went missing during this time it would be a while before anyone recognized that they were missing. By the time they were missed, it would be too late.

It took a few weeks of conditioning the girls for their new position. Once the girls were placed in a zombie state, they were taught various techniques that his customers were sure to like. Each girl was instructed on different ways and places to touch themselves. His men were given the opportunity to have sex with them publicly to make certain that the drug worked. If the drug did not work on a woman, she was dealt with quickly, and the body never found.

The demand for younger girls abroad was skyrocketing, and he wanted to stay ahead of the competition. If he played his cards right, this cash cow might never dry up. Right now, though, he was playing second fiddle; he didn't intend on being in that position for long. That was one of the reasons he decided to give this auction a try. He reviewed the numbers, and if he played his cards right, the organization would thrive as never before.

A new Family wanted to make its name known, and that didn't set well with him. How dare they think they could move in on his territory? He needed to send them a message that they were not welcome here and to move on. This was his city. Everyone answered to HIM and HIM alone!

As his clients settled down, the auctioneer started off by informing everyone the rules of the auction. He reminded them that they must wait until payment of their goods. Once they received delivery, they could do as they wished with these women. They were not allowed to touch any woman until she was paid for. As he spoke to the crowd, his authoritative voice never faltered once. The man's size also commanded attention. He stood over six feet four inches and weighed as much as a linebacker. His piercing deep brown eyes warned anyone who looked directly into his eyes not to mess with him. A goatee finished off the man's menacing look. After tonight, the Mafia Prince planned to ask this man to join his family. He was sure to move up in the ranks quickly and could be one of his better enforcers.

The Mafia Prince smiled to himself as he looked at the auctioneer. At first he feared the man may have a problem doing this when he explained what he would be auctioning off tonight. Instead, he shrugged his shoulders and asked in an impassive voice what time to be here.

After tonight, the Mafia Prince definitely had to go to confession, as would all of his men. He paid the church handsomely so that he and his men would not be turned away from confession. They all needed to unburden their souls with the sins they committed. The priest absolved them of their sins and those confessing walked away renewed once again.

Once the auctioneer finished with the rules, he looked over at the Mafia Prince and waited for further instructions. All eyes were on him, he was impervious to the world around him. This was how he maintained control. His inscrutability was what helped keep any would be disruptive buyers uncomfortable and helped bring order to what could be a chaotic event. With a quick nod of his head, his men paraded two of the girls to the stage.

As his auctioneer stared down at the crowd, they waited in silence for the bidding to start. The Mafia Prince was satisfied with his decision to use this man. Just with a stare, this man delivered a message that no amount of greed or testosterone could negate. He had the crowd under his control.

The auctioneer informed the crowd, "Gentlemen, we are ready to begin. The auction for each girl will last exactly five minutes. There is a stopwatch above the stage where everyone can see the countdown. Highest bidder wins. If you don't have the money, don't bid. If you can't pay, then we have our own ways of dealing with you and the bid will go to the next in line."

There was enthusiastic chatter among the crowd as the girls mounted the stage. The way their bodies were displayed emphasized their marketable commodities. Some of the girls best features were their breasts while others had the perfect ass. It ended up taking almost ten minutes for each girl. The Mafia Prince made a mental note to find a way to speed up the process for the next time. If not, it would take almost all night for each of the auctions. If a buyer expressed an interest in buying more than one girl, his purchases were put into a cage with his name until he was ready to leave. Some preferred to stay and watch the activities while others couldn't wait to get the girls to themselves.

Tonight's auction took longer than he expected. It was close to dawn before the auction was completed, and three girls remained unsold. He ordered that they be disposed of. None of the girls were ugly, but something about them didn't interest or attract any of the men present; he saw no reason to keep them to sell at a later date. Tonight's expenditure was efficient, orderly, and more lucrative than his wildest expectations. He'd made over two million dollars tonight alone, and they didn't even bring all the women from upstairs. He planned on having another auction in a week and needed to get busy advertising. His out of pocket expenses were almost nonexistent, which meant that the profits were astronomical. He may have hit an untapped gold mine.

Chapter 41

Alexis decided to take a walk in the moonlight while Dominic conducted business affairs inside. She wasn't in the mood tonight to listen to their incessant laughter and smell the foul cigar smoke. A gentle breeze blew off of the river and carried with it the sweet scent of star jasmine which was heavy in bloom. Fall would be here soon and they would finally have some relief from the oppressive heat that plagued the summer months.

As she returned to the house, she swatted at a mosquito that had been pestering her for the last few minutes. She knew better than to come walking out here at night, but she needed a break away from the house to clear her mind. What the private investigator talked to her about the other day on the Riverfront still weighed heavy on her mind.

She thought about asking Dominic if he had seen the young girl, but something kept stopping her. She wasn't sure why, but something told her this might not be the time to bring up the missing girl or the private investigator.

As Alexis neared the house, she saw headlights pierce through the darkness. A sleek black limousine pulled up to the house. She wondered who was arriving now. Alexis stiffened when she recognized who was stepping out of the limo. It was Frank and Alfonso Scarcelli.

Alexis moved closer to the house, not wanting anyone to see her outside. Why would Dominic lower himself to do business with that... that man?

Then Alexis began to panic. What if Frank Scarcelli wasn't here to discuss business with Dominic but had come to hurt him? She watched in fear as Frank and two of his henchmen walked up to the front door. Alexis waited in anxious anticipation as two of Dominic's workers who flanked the front door announced that the Scarcellis had arrived. Alexis stared at the scene in complete disbelief. They actually allowed Frank and Alfonso Scarcelli into their house. Alexis nervously waited for the gunfire to erupt, but instead all she heard was silence. Apprehension took over her body as she began to suspect that Dominic may, in fact, be working with the Scarcelli Family.

What if this private investigator's hunches were right? What if Dominic did have something to hide? Could Dominic be joining forces with the Scarcelli Family? Why would he want to go into business with a man like that? Alexis shook her head, trying to put the doubt she felt towards her husband out of her mind. Dominic wouldn't get mixed up in prostitution, or even worse, human trafficking, with the Scarcelli Family. Mais, his dad raised him better than that.

Yet, she was watching Frank and Alfonso Scarcelli walk into her house. Could this be why Dominic moved his meeting here rather than at the hotel? At the hotel, when Frank walked in, over seventy-five percent of the town would know in a matter of minutes that the St. Germaine Family and Scarcelli Family were meeting. It was a known fact around New Orleans, that the Scarcelli Family was nothing but trouble. They were with the Sicilian Mafia and did a lot of business with strip clubs, selling drugs and there were rumors of human trafficking.

As she stood frozen to the spot she was in, the pungent smell of Dominic's cigar tickled her nose. She looked around to notice that he had come to greet Frank with a warm handshake and a pat on the back. Alexis dropped down low, not wanting Dominic to see her outside. He thought she was up in her room relaxing and wanted to avoid the meeting. She didn't want him to know that she'd witnessed Frank and Alfonso Scarcelli walk right into her house as if the two men were best of friends.

She heard Frank tell Dominic, "Our plans have changed. We need to move up the next auction earlier than we would like. Will you have enough of the merchandise at that time?"

Dominic looked at the man and said, "I have a few now and can have my men acquire more merchandise pronto."

"Good, good."

Dread clawed at Alexis. It felt as if she was being consumed by it.

Chapter 42

Grace Arnold had been working at Café Orleans for going on six weeks, and she wasn't sure if she was cut out for this job. She was on her feet more than she liked, the tips were awful, and people always complained that the coffee was too hot. Well, if they wanted a cold coffee, then why didn't they order iced coffee? Sheesh.

She was showing a couple of tourists to the window table that overlooked the street when she saw a red Corvette careening straight for them. It didn't look like it was going to stop, and she shoved the tourists out of the way as she dove for the ground.

Grace shielded her head with her arms just as the car plowed through the window in a crashing cacophony of shattering glass and splintering wood. The car came to a stop just at the table where she was getting ready to seat the two tourists. All around her, people screamed. Someone was standing near her, but Grace had a hard time making out what he was saying. All she heard was screaming and her head was pounding. The man gave her a hand and helped her up. Someone was tending to the two tourists she'd shoved out of the way.

Grace looked at the mess and the bloodied, unconscious man at the wheel of the car, "Oh my God, what was he thinking?"

The man helping her up replied, "Mais, I don't think he knew what he was doing. It looks as if he is dead."

Grace jumped back instinctively. She had never seen a dead man, much less been in close proximity to one. Grace watched in horror as the EMT took the vitals of the man who'd caused this disaster and shook his head. Grace stood there in complete shock and disbelief. She tried to shake off the EMT as her minor cuts were tended to.

Grace swore her feet had grown roots. She didn't think she could move even if she wanted to. Her body was covered in glass and dust from head to toe. She tried to absorb the fact that she and the two tourists were almost run over by a car in the café.

She watched in dismay as the paramedics performed CPR on the man who'd caused this disaster. By the look on their face, it was a futile attempt. As one depressed on his chest, the other counted and waited for his turn to breathe into the man's bloody mouth.

Grace felt something tickling her hands; she looked down to find blood coming from a cut on the back of her hand. She started to see spots in front of her eyes, and before she knew it, darkness took over. At the sight of her blood, Grace Arnold passed out cold.

***

First Responder Timothy Hebert grew up in New Orleans and his grand-mere was a firm believer in voodoo. She was a superstitious old woman who told him the various things to look out for in the world.

When he went to check the pupils of the driver of the car, he stopped his partner, "Mais, we can't help this one, non. Someone put a voodoo hex on him. He is one of the walking dead now. He is a zombie. See how his pupils are cloudy and blank. Someone practiced black magic on this one, oui."

First Responder Chad Adams had no idea what his partner
was talking about, but he agreed that the guy's pupils were
like nothing he had ever seen. "Dude, you buy into that
voodoo shit? Mais, this guy isn't the walking dead; he is just
dead."

Hebert shook his head, "Mais, I am telling you right now
that this man is a zombie, the walking dead. I need to call
my grand-mere and ask if she knows how to cure this man.
There has to be an antidote of some kind."

After letting the phone ring enough times for his grand-
mere to answer the phone, he explained what happened.
He informed his partner, "What we are about to do is
completely unorthodox and I need to know if you will back
me up with this before we leave."

Chad looked at his partner, unsure of what he was about to
ask, "Before we bring this man to the hospital, we need to
stop by my grand-mere's house. She will see if someone
put a hex on him. If anyone can help him, it will be her."

"I don't know dude. This could land us into a lot of trouble."

Shrugging is shoulders, he stated, "By all accounts, this guy
is dead and everyone here will think we are taking him to
the hospital. If we do take him to the hospital, I don't think
anyone there can save him. However, my grand-mere may
be able to. If nothing else, she can confirm if my suspicions
are right."

"Is it at least on the way?"

"Mais oui. It won't take us off course. We have to pass by
her home on the way to the hospital."

"All right then, let's go see if your grand-mere will tell you that you are nuts before heading to the hospital. I sure hope you are right and this man doesn't die on us before we get to the hospital."

As they loaded him up into the ambulance, Hebert replied, "I will take full responsibility."

Chapter 43

Teresa walked into the spa for her monthly waxing. She considered going through the laser treatment to remove her unwanted hair, but something about the pain turned her on. Besides, her man liked her bare assets and she would do anything to please him.

Teresa grew up wealthy, and always had the finer things in life. Since coming to America, she had found so many more things she could do with her husband's money and lucky for her, he never said no to anything she wanted. That could be because her mother taught her how to manipulate men at an early age as well as being conniving. Even if Teresa's father did tell her mother no, she found a way to defy him without him ever knowing.

Teresa wished he would listen to her mother and even to her; a woman could run The Family business just as well as a man. Yet, he refused to listen to them. That was when Teresa's mom devised her own plan and put the wheels in motion.

Teresa had yet to convince him that she could control the affluent empire. For now, she must sit at the side of her husband's throne. Luckily, her husband had a vast empire of his own that was being merged with her family. A rush of anticipation flowed through her body as she thought of what their net worth would be when everything was finalized. The net worth would be in the billions of dollars. In both America and Italy, that was a substantial amount of money.

Teresa couldn't find fault with her husband. He made sure she wanted for nothing and unlike her father, gave her freedom to roam about the United States shopping as she wished. She was quickly learning how to be a socialite and a kept wife here in New Orleans. Alfonso even let her host a few dinner parties as well as attend several charity functions around town. Teresa loved to be seen around town with him on her arm. What's more important was that she was seen with whatever new piece of jewelry she had found to wear for that function. Back home, her father hadn't been fond of Teresa or her mother wasting money on materialistic things. They were both given a generous weekly allowance, but nothing more than what he gave them. Teresa found what he gave them was never enough for the purchases she desired. Now, she had an unlimited cash flow and plenty of time to go shopping.

Alfonso didn't even ask where she was going as she'd headed out this morning. She sometimes wondered if he had her every movement traced which was why he never asked where she was going. Although if he were having her followed, she probably wouldn't be alive right now. No, he must be a fool and trusted her completely. He never asked where she had been when she walked into the house after he had clearly been home for a while. Instead, he merely smiled and continued on with whatever he was doing. The marriage was perfect for him. When he needed a piece of ass, he climbed into her bed. Other than that, he let her indulge in whatever she wanted to. He had never said anything about her spontaneous vacations or numerous shopping trips. He spoiled her unconditionally. He treated her like a princess, but she had a feeling that would come to an end shortly. She would do whatever it took to maintain the lifestyle she had become accustomed to.

After she was done at the spa, she stopped by a lingerie shop and picked up a new nightie before heading to the hotel. She couldn't wait to see her lover. The marriage may have helped her family, but her lover would help her future. She hoped to make it to the hotel room before he did. She wanted to change into her new nightie for him.

When she unlocked the hotel room door, she knew instantly that he was already there. The room was dark except for a few candles he'd lit. He must be in a romantic mood as well. So much for turning him on with the new nightie, but there was always next time.

As she closed and locked the door with the do not disturb sign showing, she felt his strong arms embrace her. Alfonso may work out religiously, but his physique would never compete with her lover's and while Alfonso may be good in bed he didn't compare to her lover. No, her lover knew all the right moves that turned her on with just a simple look and touch.

With his very touch, raw desire shot right through her. When his hands moved down her body closer to her womanhood, desire erupted deep inside of her and turned her blood into molten lava. She couldn't get enough of his touch.

He kissed her with so much passion; she melted into him. She no longer felt the doorknob pressing into her back. All she cared about was him and how his kisses ignited her blood. He turned her around abruptly and blindfolded her. He whispered, "I want you to concentrate on nothing but my touch."

He made her feel whole in his arms. She couldn't see him, but she could smell him and feel his arms wrapped around her as he carried her to the bed.

He picked her up and placed her down on the bed. Then his hands were everywhere. She was quickly aroused. Again, he whispered in her ear, "Spread your legs for me. I want to see all of you."

She did as he said, not bothering to question his motives. The mental images of what he was doing to her body were a huge turn on. One of his masterful hands cupped her generous breast as the other hand made its way down her body. Every single nerve inside of her sizzled in an unquenchable heat. He continued to stroke her, delving even deeper inside of her. She felt as if she would burst into flames from the desire racing through her body. When his thumb caressed her most sensitive spot, she couldn't hold back the convulsions. She shuddered hard against his finger, but he never stopped. He continued to thrust his finger inside of her as if he was stoking a fire. His touch sent aftershocks through her body.

Before she knew what he was doing, he took her hand and placed it where his hand just left. "I want to see you touch yourself. Do this for me."

She tentatively touched herself, unsure of what he wanted. When she heard his breath quicken as her finger slid inside of her, she found exhilaration like never before. She smiled to herself and continued to rub herself.

He kissed her with such a hunger that it devoured her. His kiss was hard and all consuming. His teeth closed over her bottom lip and nipped at it ever so gently.

***

When she kissed him back with the same amount of passion, need for her coursed through him like an explosion waiting to happen. When she reached down and touched him, that need exploded into unbridled desire. He flipped her over and let her straddle his body. He wanted to feel her hands on him, her mouth all over his body. As she moved down his body, she let out a seductive laugh. He wasn't sure how much longer of her teasing he could take. When her mouth found his erection, he lost all conscious thought of anything else.

Her mouth teased him to no end. She slowly circled his tip and licked his hard shaft before taking as much of him as she could into her mouth. He let her ministrations go on until he thought he would burst. He pulled her up to him and kissed her hard with raw passion. He needed to be deep inside of her. He flipped her over in one swift movement and plunged into her.

***

As Teresa lay satisfied next to her lover, she knew she should feel guilty. He must have sensed what was on her mind and pulled her closer, "We can end this you know."

She shook her head, "I know I should feel guilty, but I don't. It's not like we have a conventional marriage. Besides, he probably doesn't even realize I am not home right now. He lets me do as I please as long as he can run his business the way he wants to. Hell, he is usually away from home on various business trips and I never see him."

He pulled her close, "If you were mine, I wouldn't let you out of my sight. You are an exquisite woman with an insatiable appetite that I find thrilling."

As they parted ways, she wondered if he knew her exact plans for him. He was not only useful in bed, but also for her to accomplish her dream.

Chapter 44

Guy Mayon was confident that Dominic St. Germaine had something to do with these missing women from around the area. He had yet to convince the wife of his involvement. He wondered what such an attractive woman as herself even saw in a man like him.

The deeper he dug into St. Germaine's past the more he became convinced the man was dirty. If his suspicions were correct, St. Germaine was part of the Mafia problem plaguing this city. If that were the case, then that would explain why the cops turned a blind eye to the missing girls' reports. He wondered how much of this town the St. Germaine Family had on their payroll. For a blind eye to be turned on so many missing girls, the pockets must run deep.

From what he'd heard around town, there were three families that could be involved in the missing girl cases and he had yet to confirm that the Devereaux Family or Scarcelli Family was involved. Although, he received word that the FBI was indeed looking into the Scarcelli Family's involvement in possible human trafficking. He had kept a close eye on Dominic St. Germaine and the Scarcelli Family. He hadn't found any evidence that the Devereaux Family was involved with the missing girls, but he did let the FBI know he believed they might be part of the mob problem here. He had seen a few known drug traffickers in and out of some of their businesses. He heard a few people refer to Alfonso Scarcelli as The Mafia Prince. Then yesterday, he heard someone refer to how Dominic St. Germaine was still called The Mafia Prince and should change his nickname to Boss. His suspicions that St. Germaine was Mafia may be well founded.

His best chance of obtaining more information on Dominic St. Germaine may involve talking to his wife again. The last time they spoke, he may have broken through some of that barrier she'd built around herself regarding her husband. For a moment he saw a light bulb go off in her head. Something he said clicked with her, but what was it? She dismissed him so fast that he wasn't sure what he said that scared her off. Could it be mentioning one of the missing girls worked at her husband's strip club? Did she not know he owned a strip club and certain warehouses on the port?

Guy had tried to get near the warehouses on the port for the past month, but the goon squad was unusually thick there. His gut told him that was where they were hiding these girls, but without further evidence, he couldn't be sure.

Guy was determined to find out what was happening to these girls. There was a chance he was about to stumble upon something huge, and as much as he hated to enlist the help of an innocent, bringing in Alexis St. Germaine may be his only way.

Chapter 45

It was Brian's turn to watch the girls. This was the part of the job that he despised. He could pass some time by having fun with any of the girls, but screwing an unconscious girl didn't get a rise out of him. The girls were kept in a drugged stupor to keep them controllable.

Brian had no problems killing someone who owed his Boss money, but this new business venture still didn't sit too well with him. He did as instructed as he prized his life. If he kept building up the Boss's trust in him, he would continue making rank in the Family. If all went well, one day soon he would be the underboss, or better the cleaner.

As he made his rounds, he checked in on the girls once more. He had a strong suspicion his Boss's voodoo priestess was using some of that black magic she did on these girls. They looked just like the slaves utilized in the sweat shops. Hell, Brian wasn't even sure if turning those that couldn't pay into zombies was better than killing them. They just stared out into space and took the orders the voodoo priestess gave them. She had complete control over them, or so she said. They still had to make sure they kept them shackled, so they didn't wander off. He let one go free by accident, and before he knew it, the blasted thing had walked off. It took forever to find the damn thing and then when he did, it lunged for him. No matter how hard he struck the thing, it didn't register that he should feel pain.

Once Brian made his rounds, he met his Boss back at the small office and told him goodbye. Brian watched as his Boss and bodyguards left for the night. His new bodyguard was built like a damn linebacker. The man had muscles on his muscles. He wondered if he took steroids to give him that much mass. When age caught up with him, he would be in trouble. All that muscle would more than likely turn to fat.

After they had left, he made sure everything was locked up and turned on some music. The warehouse was soon filled with the sounds of a current popular pop song. While the beat of the music pulsed through him, he pulled out his cocaine. Normally, he didn't like to take drugs while working, but sitting here watching these zombified girls was hardly work.

He shook out a line of cocaine on the back of his hand and inhaled it. He closed his eyes and felt his body relax as the drugs entered his system. Even the music seemed to flow through his blood. He kicked his feet up on the desk and let the drug induced feeling take over his body.

He had to rub his eyes to make sure what he was seeing wasn't a figment of his imagination.

***

Alexis watched as Dominic and his goons left the warehouse. Being careful to stay in the shadows, she worked her way to the door. While Dominic showered last night, she'd swiped his key chain. She doubted he would even notice it missing as he had someone else open doors for him, usually Brian. After trying a few keys, she finally unlocked the door and peered inside.

What she saw there was beyond her worst fears. She was frozen in fear at the sight in front of her. How could the man she loved do this? The man she loved was better than this. She never imagined he was capable of something this cruel.

Alexis was horrified. In front of her were young girls, some barely teenagers. They were caged like animals, arms and legs shackled. They looked as if they were drugged, no one moved. A blanket was thrown on the floor for them to lie on and nothing else.

What would possess Dominic to do something like this? He was raised to respect women, not to demoralize them. A noise from the corner caught her attention. Out of the shadows appeared Brian, Dominic's right hand man. She swallowed down her fear, unsure of what he would do to her.

Without thinking, she backed up and found herself against the door. Using more force than he needed, Brian grabbed her and drug her over to his corner office.

He demanded, "What the hell do you think you're doing? Does Dominic know that you are here?" She watched in horror as he picked up his phone, "No, of course he doesn't. You know curiosity killed the cat."

The whole time he was talking, he waved his gun around. He removed some duct tape from his desk and restrained her.

Once Alexis was restrained to the chair, he called Dominic, "Boss we have a slight problem at the warehouse. You need to head over here again."

Dominic let out a deep sigh. "We don't have a problem with badges do we?"

"Mais non, Boss. Badges I can handle. I would never bring you in the middle of that. This is something that you will want to handle as you see fit."

Dominic informed him, "I will be there shortly."

A shiver ran through Alexis as Brian glared at her. There was pure evil in his eyes, "Your husband is on his way. You better get your story straight."

When Dominic entered the warehouse, Alexis had hot tears running down her face. He smiled and grabbed her chin. He forced her to look into his eyes. There was so much rage and hate there. It was an expression that she'd never seen from him before. One that she couldn't imagine even the most heartless and cold criminal making. She had no idea what he was capable of. As the tears continued to flow and blur her vision, her body convulsed in fear. Nausea welled up in her stomach and moved up her throat. She feared that he would kill her.

Dominic suddenly stopped pacing and looked directly at Alexis. He could see the fear in her eyes. He asked her, "Why? Why did you have to come here? Now that you have seen what is going on, something will have to be done. You can't be trusted to keep this quiet."

Alexis looked up at him with tears glittering in her eyes, "Why? Why must you do this?"

Out of the shadows stepped Bianca. Alexis stared at her in utter disbelief, "Now, Alexis surely you must know about Dominic's business dealings?"

Alexis shook her head, "No, Dominic couldn't be involved in this." She looked at Dominic with denial written on her face, "Did she talk you into this? Dominic this isn't you?"

Bianca stepped closer to Alexis, "Oh, but my pet, this is Dominic. There are things that you don't know about your husband that would turn your stomach."

Alexis watched in horror as Bianca put her arms around Dominic and kissed him with raw passion. Alexis looked at Dominic, "What is going on here Dominic?"

Dominic pushed Bianca out of the way, "Alexis, you have to understand that this is just business. I never meant for you to find out about any of this, but now that you have, I can't let you tell anyone either."

Dominic looked over at Bianca, "I want this to be quick and painless, do you understand me. No voodoo curses and no suffering." Dominic looked over at Brian, "Make sure she doesn't suffer. I can't bear to watch this."

***

Brian saw this as an opportune moment. This would have him making rank in the family. He could see himself sitting at the right hand of the Boss. And if something unfortunate should happen to him, then Brian would be the one to take over. Especially, now that the wife would be taken care of before she could give him any heirs. Dominic may think he was indestructible, but he was messing with fire when he played with his voodoo priestess. If she found out what he did behind her back, then she would put some kind of voodoo curse on him.

Alexis started to scream at the top of her lungs, "You don't have to do this Dominic. I promise I won't say a word."

As Bianca moved closer to her, Alexis spat in her face, "My parents will wonder where I am. I will be missed."

Dominic turned back to Alexis with a venomous look, "Your parents know better than to question me, or they will suffer the same fate. Your dad has worked with my Family for years now. Why do you think our marriage was arranged?

Your dad had no male heirs and wanted to combine forces with the St. Germaines.”

Bianca glared down at Alexis with triumph clearly showing in her eyes, “Don't worry cher. At least you won't suffer the same fate as the others that crossed Dominic.”

“What… What do you mean?”

“There are worse things than death; you can be the walking dead.”

Alexis tried to hide the tremble in her voice, “Walking dead?”

“I have a potion that has you walking the earth where you are not quite alive, but not dead either.”

Bianca stepped closer to Alexis and brushed the tears off of her face, “But then again, you have such a pretty bone structure that maybe we can use you in some of our potions. Some are killed and boiled down to the bone. Then I take their bones and pulverize them to sell. We make a small fortune off of the voodoo items. People pay a lot for something they think will give them magical powers.”

Bianca pointed to the girls in the cage, “Count yourself lucky that you won't be joining these girls. They will be sold.”

“What do you mean sold?”

Bianca let out a maniacal laugh, “We sell girls worldwide. Thanks to the internet and the right connections no one will ever know what happened to them. The younger girls fetch a pretty penny too.”

***

Alexis was rigid with fear at the various things they could do to her and none pleasant. Her heart went out to these girls held captive. When they killed Alexis, her torture would be over, but theirs would be just beginning. That was if they killed her, she was still unsure of what her fate would be.

***

Guy Mayon could smell the adrenaline in the air as the SWAT van drove to the warehouse. It took some convincing for his friend, Detective Mike Bailey, to grant him permission to attend the raid. Mike handpicked those who would be included in the raid. There was a lot riding on this, and it could prove to be fatal for all involved if the information fell into the wrong hands.

Everyone was decked out in full body armor. Guy hoped that the warehouse was minimally guarded and that the armor and weapons were overkill. No one was briefed on the full scope of the raid until they were in the van. If Alexis was correct, then Dominic had friends in very high places and they would let him know about the raid immediately.

As the van stopped and the doors opened, Guy took in several deep breaths and readied himself. He stepped in place at the end of the line of officers as they moved out. The windows were too high to see what was on the inside.

There were no cars parked near the warehouse and by the look of it, the warehouse appeared to be vacant.

The SWAT team split into two groups. The first group headed towards the front of the warehouse while the second group headed to the loading dock in the back. The leader of Guy's group used a small mirror to check the front of the warehouse. He signaled that they were clear to move in.

***

Bianca and Brian both heard the proximity alarm go off. She exclaimed to Brian, "Grab my hand. We must get out of here now." Using her transposing spell, they departed the warehouse just as the doors were blasted open.

Alexis couldn't believe her eyes. The two vanished into thin air.

Chapter 46

Teresa snuggled against Alfonso and listened to him sleep. She smiled as she thought about the ride she'd just given him. She looked at the alarm clock on the nightstand to check the time. She was too excited to sleep. Soon they would put their plan into action. She still couldn't believe that no one had yet found out about her and her lover.

Her lover wanted a voodoo priestess to use black magic, but Teresa wanted him to see the betrayal before he died. It took some coercing to convince him this was the best way to handle this matter before he finally gave in to her demands. To make sure he didn't change his mind, she used an incantation she found. It was one of Marie Laveau's spells on how to drive someone to murder. It had to be done at just the right time for the incantation to work. The hardest ingredient for her to get was the alligator brain, but she finally found it and then performed the incantation.

As the clock struck midnight, she heard the sound of footsteps on the stairs. Instinctively, Alfonso reached for his gun that wasn't there. She asked him to leave it in the dresser this one time, just as she had asked him to let his bodyguards have the night off. She resorted to tears, pleading with him for one night of normalcy. She reminded him that no one would ever attempt anything on him, that he was too feared. After he agreed to her pleas, she realized she was getting better at convincing these strong men to bend to her every wish. She wondered if her lover knew what she had in mind for him as well. Why must a man run the Mafia? These chauvinistic pigs never once considered that a woman could do the job. Even her dad fretted and married her off because he did not have a male son to take over the business. He never considered her for the job.

Since arriving in America, she had discovered voodoo. Listening to her lover talk about how he used voodoo in his Family, she learned as much as she could on the subject. She may not be as powerful as Bianca Honore, who had been studying all of her life, but she was quite powerful with spells. With a little more practice, she would be a force to reckon with. No one would ever suspect her as being the one performing the rituals.

Teresa wore her charm to protect herself from Bianca and anyone else who may want to stop her from performing the black arts of voodoo. She doubted Bianca even suspected it was her. No one would suspect an outsider. She feared since she wasn't born into voodoo that she wouldn't be able to perform the black magic, but an old lady informed her that it wasn't about who you were but about what was in your heart. For voodoo to work, you must honestly believe in it. Once she opened her mind and body to it, she found that the first small potions and spells that she made worked. This gave her courage to try harder incantations and spells. She was ready to move on to the more dangerous of black magic. She had been making special voodoo dolls. It took some trickery to get a lock of hair from Bianca and her lover, but soon they would know what she planned for them.

As the gunman barged into the room, Teresa let out a blood curdling scream for good measure. The intruder calmly pointed the assault rifle at the two lying in bed. She prepared herself for the sound of gunfire that was soon to come. Before Alfonso could ask what the intruder wanted, the sound of the gun's blast rang through the room. A bullet struck Alfonso between his eyes.

As the blood flowed down her dead husband's face, she got up off the bed and ran to her lover. As she leapt into his arms, she pulled off his ski mask and gave him a deep kiss. He held her tightly, kissing her back.

He looked deep into her eyes, "You know when his father hears of this, there will be hell to pay."

She smiled up at him, "It is time you let your voodoo priestess see how far her black magic reaches."

The Mafia Prince laughed, "I love the way you think."

Her momma would be proud when she heard how well the plan was going. Soon she would be the one everyone feared.

Chapter 47

In the fog that came rolling in off of the mighty river, a figure took form. At first the features were vague and merely drifted along with the fog. Dominic watched in fascination as the figure took shape. He could make out her long flowing white gown and auburn hair that streamed across her back. Occasionally, the breeze delicately picked up her hair and moved it. She seemed to make her way to him, casting no shadow from the fog obscured moon.

He heard Bianca approaching him and informed her, "Do you see her? It can't be her?"

Bianca peered into the fog, trying to see what he was pointing to. He asked her once more, "Please tell me you see her. She is right there. You can see her moving towards us."

***

Bianca once more peered deep into the dense fog, trying to see what Dominic saw. For a moment, she thought she saw something move in the fog. She shook her head, not wanting to believe that she was out there. But then, she saw the movement once again. There was a figure in the mist. Her auburn hair was picked up by the wind and flowed behind her. She watched as the figure stopped and just stared at them. Then the figure disappeared in the whirling clouds of fog. Bianca repeatedly blinked, trying to see if she could find the figure in the fog once again.

She shook her head and told Dominic, "It is just a figment of your imagination. The fog is thick as pea soup tonight."

He looked at Bianca in disbelief, "You saw her, didn't you? You aren't scared?"

Bianca shook her head, but kept peering into the dense fog waiting to see if the figure appeared once more. There was nothing there.

***

Dominic heard footsteps approaching from behind. He turned to see his mother coming out of the house. Even at this hour, she looked completely made up. Her hair was still tucked in a tight chignon, not a hair out of place. She had yet to dress for the night and still wore her dress and high heels.

Even now she still looked at ease, serene almost. "What are you doing out here Dominic?"

He bent down and kissed his mother on the cheek, "I wanted some fresh air before bed."

Bianca looked intently at mother and son. There was no doubt of their lineage. Dominic inherited his looks from his mother, but as much as he tried to deny it, he had his dad's temperament. Dominic's mother attempted to instill a calmer temperament in Dominic, but at times, she could see the venom that ran in his blood. He was a man to be feared.

Dominic led his mother back inside, not wanting to share his fears that Alexis wandered these grounds. After all, no one knew she was dead except Brian and Bianca and both of them would not be talking.

Once inside, he continued to peer into the fog. Maybe it was just a figment of his imagination. There was nothing there except fog and shadows. His mother touched his shoulder, "Dominic you should go to bed. It is getting late and I am sure you have a busy day ahead of you."

Dominic looked at his mother and nodded, "I plan on going to bed soon, but first I must see Bianca out."

As Dominic walked Bianca to the front door, he caught a whiff of Cuban cigars. He looked around to see where the smell was coming from. Bianca noticed his unease, "What is it, cher?"

"Do you smell that?"

"Someone must have been smoking a cigar earlier is all."

He shook his head, "Mais non, that is my dad. The ghosts must be restless tonight, but why? Has my dad come here to tell me something?"

"Ah cher, the ghosts aren't restless. I am sure that someone had a cigar, and the smell of it is still lingering. You have to trust me; I would know if the spirits were restless tonight."

He let out a sigh, "I guess you are right. It's just I swear when the fog rolled in, I saw Alexis walking about, and now the smell of dad's cigars is heavy in the air. It makes one wonder."

Bianca took his hand in hers, "You are working too hard. You need to relax."

Dominic knew that she was correct. She would sense that the spirits were restless.

***

The ghost of Rayne Simoneaud watched as Bianca and Dominic headed back into the house. A sinister smile formed across her face. She had only just begun to haunt these two.

Chapter 48

Now that Dominic's plans were falling into place all he had to do was end his relationship with Bianca. It had been great, but now that he was with Teresa he must play his cards carefully. He had not yet told Teresa about Bianca and vice versa.

As he lay in bed, he watched as Bianca stretched languidly. He may be a cad after all since he decided to have one more fling with her before ending it. He had not yet given Teresa a taste of what he truly desired for fear of putting a halt to his plans. So far, Teresa had played right into his hands and fallen for everything hook line and sinker. Until they were married, though, he would have to watch what he did. He needed to wait a few more days before reporting his wife missing. It had been perfect when she found out his dirty little secret; Bianca was more than willing to rid him of his wife. However, Bianca felt that she would be his next wife, and he needed to rectify that quickly. He would find out from Brian where Alexis's body was located and frame Bianca for her murder. That would rid him of Bianca. She would look like a scorned lover who eliminated the competition. When Teresa married Alfonso, the two families combined to become a force to be reckoned with. With Alfonso no longer in the picture, he and Teresa would rule the three families with no one to stop them. Frankie Scarcelli met his demise right after his son met his. Everything was planned perfectly.

He turned over and looked at Bianca, "We need to talk."

Bianca looked at him with concern in her eyes, "Mais, what do we need to talk about. With your wife gone, you are free to see me now."

He kissed her on the lips before replying, "I have had a change in plans. I am seeing Teresa Scarcelli. We are going to combine the Families."

Bianca jumped out of the bed, anger seething from her very skin. Even angry, this woman was exquisite. There was something so alluring about the way the moonlight shimmered off of her body. She paced back and forth in the large room that he and Alexis had shared.

Mumbling more to herself than to him, she exclaimed, "I knew that I shouldn't have fallen for you. I should have ended this a long time ago, when my powers were already strong. I should have known that you were a snake in the grass and were just using me."

She looked at him with rage in her eyes. He knew she was waiting for a response, but nothing he said would make this any easier. She moved to the foot of the bed and glared down at him, "See even now you have nothing to say. What is your new girlfriend hoping to do? Does she want to move into here as soon as possible? Does she know that you ordered the death of your wife? Mais, I wonder if your new girlfriend knows about your appetites."

Dominic tried to calm her, "Cher, I do care about you. It's just that right now we need to keep things quiet. I don't want to scare Teresa off until everything is finalized. Do you know how big this Family will be? It will combine three Families. When Teresa married Alfonso Scarcelli it merged two powerful Families, one here in America and one in Italy. With Frankie and Alfonso Scarcelli out of the way, I can merge with Teresa and we will dominate the south as well as Italy."

She glared at him and then paced once again, "Your problem is that you want too much power. You are letting greed over take you and forgetting those who helped you get here. You can't use me and then push me aside. You think you can get everything you want with just a wave of your hand because of who you are?"

He reminded her, "You wanted power just as much as me. I seem to recall you wanted to become the Voodoo Queen of New Orleans cher."

Bianca didn't like having the fact that she used him to get what she wanted thrown in her face. Maybe, they did use each other to some degree, but she cared for him. How dare he treat her like this!

Chapter 49

Dominic bolted upright in bed. He reached for the bedspread that he'd kicked off in the middle of the night. It felt as if the temperature in the room dropped drastically. A sense of foreboding washed over him. He swore there was someone in the room with him. He looked around to see if anyone was there.

Suddenly a heaviness came across him. If he didn't know better, he would think he was having a heart attack. His blood ran cold; a figure emerged from the darkness. This had to be his imagination. The woman was dead yet here she stood just as beautiful as the night Bianca gave her the kiss of death.

Even in death, her ethereal beauty showed. He shook his head to clear the image in front of him. Even after blinking his eyes, she remained in his room. She had yet to look at him, but he knew it was her. Her hair shimmered in the moonlight as she paced back and forth. Even in the darkness, he could make out her voluptuous body underneath the sheer nightgown. The nightgown clung to her curves in all the right places. His heart caught in his throat as he made out the bump in her belly. He shook his head, this couldn't be. Could it be that Bianca didn't kill her and she had been waiting for the perfect time to make her presence known?

Then she looked at Dominic, and he felt his heart stop beating. Her once gorgeous green eyes were now black as night. It seemed as if time stood still as their eyes locked on each other. He watched in horror as her mouth opened to speak, but no sound came out, just a vile smell. It reminded

him of death and decay. No, this couldn't be happening.
This must be a nightmare.

Instinctively, he reached for the Gris Gris bag he kept under
his pillow. Thankfully, he had enough common sense to
have a special bag made for him before venturing into the
voodoo business. The lady had told him to make sure that
no other person touched his Gris Gris bag. To do so would
cause the bag to lose its power.

***

Rayne Simoneaud's eyes flared with rage at the sight of the
man who'd betrayed her. Rayne disappeared from the
room as easily as she'd appeared. Whatever Bianca had in
store for this one was far worse than anything Rayne could
do. She would seek out her revenge on Brian before turning
on Bianca. She must gather her strength to fight Bianca.
Rayne had already seen where Bianca had relocated her
zombies and followers deep in the swamp.

Her new home was a primitive dwelling. It was constructed
of cypress and heavily covered with Spanish moss. The hut
was built on stilts with a rope ladder being the only way up.
Several other huts were constructed on the ground for her
followers and the zombies. Rayne needed to keep a close
eye on Bianca.

Chapter 50

The airport was crowded. Travelers rushed along the busy corridors with a set purpose, to get somewhere. Alexis listened to the wheels of the other travelers' luggage making a whirling noise across the floor. A monotonous male voice echoed through the terminal giving instructions for lost bags and gate changes.

Guy Mayon stood beside her waiting for their turn to board the plane. They both kept an eye out for any of Dominic's henchmen. He kept one hand firmly on her elbow in case he needed to direct her in another direction quickly. Her heart hadn't stopped pounding since that fateful night he rescued her. She still had no idea how they had escaped with their very lives or the lives of those girls that were being held captive, but they did. Each of the girls held captive had been returned to their homes or had been relocated where they no longer had to worry about Dominic or Bianca.

Alexis still couldn't believe any of this was real. She was running for her life. He glanced down at her and his eyes showed such strength and confidence.

She didn't know if she could find that strength inside of her. Her whole world seemed to be coming to an end. What would happen to her? What would Dominic do to her family? Would he kill them for retribution or would he keep eyes and ears on them in case she tried to contact them?

She couldn't take her eyes off of the various passengers; always fearing one of them was hired by Dominic to take care of her. There were so many different types of people here. Some had long flowing hair while others had short hair and others were even bald. There were some overweight and some that looked anorexic. Each person had some place they were going. Each person here had their own hopes and dreams waiting to be realized. Her hopes and dreams came crashing to an end that night in the warehouse. Dominic's hatred for her became evident when she went looking for answers to her questions in his warehouse; she saw where she fit into his world. He'd planned to get rid of her that very night.

***

Guy looked down at his damsel in distress. Her complexion was still pale, almost gray. It was almost as if her spirit was taken from her. He wondered if that voodoo priestess managed to work a spell on her. Her eyes were lifeless, the rims red and bloodshot. He asked, "Are you okay?"

***

Trying to sound unaffected by everything that happened, she replied, "I'm getting there."

As Alexis headed out into the unknown, she prayed that the rumors were true and that Dominic had been arrested. Still, she didn't feel safe knowing that he was behind bars. Thankfully, Guy Mayon listened to her pleas to not let the cops know that she was alive. Her husband had many friends in not only the New Orleans Police Department but she was fairly certain the FBI as well. No, she would take her chances keeping herself hidden. She was grateful she had enough sense to hide money when she witnessed him doing business with the Scarcellis. Money would do her no good if she was dead, but at least now she would be able to hide in comfort. She had not yet told Guy Mayon that she had more than enough money to live on. She was fairly sure that she could trust him, but she was not one hundred percent certain. Until she was sure, she would keep the money well hidden.

As they prepared to board the plan, a news report flashed across the screen. It appeared Dominic's betrayal went further than she realized. Not only was he having several affairs on her, but he was sleeping with Scarcelli's wife. They were both arrested in his death. Alexis smiled at the thought of everything Bianca was liable to do to the man now that his betrayal was known. The prison system would not permit him to keep his little Gris Gris bag. Bianca would be planning her revenge soon.

Even with Dominic's arrest, there was no reason for her to stay. All that remained here were bad memories. It was time for her to start a new life, somewhere far away from here. With Guy Mayon's help, she planned on doing just that.

Epilogue

The midday sun burned bright outside the small primitive hut that Bianca now called home. Thin, bony fingers reached out from the shadows turning the voodoo doll in all directions. Large green eyes began to glow red as the hatred took over her body. A sinister smile formed on her face.

She moved the doll's arms to the highest position until they were way above its head, then lowered to reach out in front as if in a pleading application. This was how she imagined Dominic sitting in front of her, begging and pleading for his miserable life.

Hard, strong fingers gripped the waist of the doll, almost squeezing him in two before relaxing. Next, she took a pin and dipped it into a small bowl of blood and pushed it deep into the voodoo doll's chest, making sure to avoid any internal organs. This ritual was repeated four more times. Blood began to ooze from the doll. A maniacal laughter filled the small room as she imagined Dominic St. Germaine falling to the floor in agony.

Finally, she slowly pushed the pin covered in blood and her special potion into his heart as she recited her incantation.

***

As soon as Dominic felt the first tightening in his chest, he dropped to his knees and said the Hail Mary. By the time the guards heard his guttural screams of agony, they were too late. They stood back in horror and watched as the man grabbed his chest and fell to the floor dead.

At the neighboring women's correctional facility, Teresa Scarcelli suffered the same fate moments later.

Thank you!

Dear Reader,

Thank you for purchasing this book. I hope you enjoyed reading this novel as much as I enjoyed writing it.

It is very important for me to hear what you think about the book. Your reviews give me inspiration in my future writings. You can leave a review on Amazon, Goodreads or Barnes and Noble.

Your thoughts and opinions mean a lot to me.

Please enjoy a sample of Seduced By Voodoo. The battle of good versus evil will soon take place in the bayous of New Orleans, Louisiana. The foolish mortals thought they could stop her. However, Bianca Honore with her new vampire lover, Joshua, will raise an army of the living dead. Can Father Mark Trahan stop this ever growing evil before it is too late?

Also, be sure to check out my website and social media sites for upcoming books and giveaways.

Sincerely,

Mary Theriot

Links

Website www.maryreasontheriot.com

Goodreads for reviews
http://www.goodreads.com/MaryReasonTheriot

Facebook - http://goo.gl/Sd0VgY

Twitter - @Mktheriot

Google+ - +MaryTheriot

YouTube - http://goo.gl/ErM1M6

Pinterest - http://www.pinterest.com/mktheriot

Blog Page, www.maryreasontheriot.me

Seduced by Voodoo

****

By: Mary Reason Theriot

Prologue

They came in the dark of the night. They came when man remained alone, forced to face his failures and fears, when man's horrors and atrocities could be shown to them. This was when the frightening and unexplainable would appear.

It was time for creatures that went bump in the night to awaken. As the dark heavens peeled back, a glowing orange moon was revealed. Evil lurked about in the darkness of the night. This was when mortals found out exactly what walked amongst them. This was where horror and mystery made its appearance.

Of all the supernatural beings, there was one to be most feared. Vampires were a pariah even amongst demons. They were the most foul and barbaric of what walked this earth or were they? Or was there something worse that walked this earth?

Chapter 1

Detective Grace Hutcherson never considered falling in love. Yet, she was falling completely head over heels for Detective Mike Bailey. She couldn't get over how falling in love changed your view of the world.

Hell, she never even looked for love. Somehow, it found her. Fate stepped in and set in motion the chain of events over the last few months that led up to her meeting Mike Bailey. Right now, she was putty in cupid's hands.

Fate never asked if she wanted to fall in love. It simply decided that she needed Mike to fill the hole in her heart.

She had never felt like this for another human being and now here she was aching to be in Mike's arms once again. Her world bloomed with that beautiful never ending ache. Now that she had fallen in love with Mike Bailey, she couldn't imagine her life without him.

She feared for Mike's life, though. The vampire escaped and kept intruding upon her thoughts. She saw what happened to people in his way. It was funny how fate worked. Fate brought the vampire and Mike into her life and now they were all intertwined. She prayed that the vampire would soon be out of her life so that she and Mike could enjoy their new found love.

She didn't know what she would do without Mike. He was the gravity that kept her center aligned. Without him in her life, she would be adrift in this world without a compass.

Grace woke this morning with a sense of foreboding. She was bleakly certain that something would happen today and she prayed that it did not involve anyone she knew or loved.

The master vampire attempted to infiltrate her thoughts once again last night. No matter how hard she tried to block him from her mind, he still managed to do so. He sensed her ability to read his mind and used it to his advantage. She detested the fact that he could invade her mind and read her thoughts.

Something was off about today; she could feel it in her bones. From the very moment she roused this morning, her instincts were on alert and they were never wrong. Before the vampire started invading her thoughts, she only saw visions after they happened. She could never predict the future, but lately, she felt a calamity barreling straight for her and she had no idea what it could be.

She wished she knew more about this gift of perception and insight that she had. If this was such a wonderful gift, then she should have been given the ability to change what was about to come. How could she ward off a disaster if she didn't know what it was, when it would happen or where it was coming from?

As she locked her front door and headed to her car, she looked around the street. A sensation that someone was watching her every movement washed over her. Perhaps she was letting her imagination get away from her. There was no immediate threat lurking in the shadows just waiting to make a move. Still, she couldn't shake the feeling that came from deep inside of her.

She leaned against her car and stared up into the sky. Maybe looking into the cloudless expanse of blue would give her some answers. Letting out a sigh, if only the answer would come to her.

She should be truthful with herself, she was nothing more than a scared animal, one that sensed an impending earthquake coming and ran around frantically looking for shelter. Whatever was coming for her, she would not be able to outrun it. No, she would have to stay and fight whatever it was.

As she settled behind the wheel of her car, she caught her reflection in the rearview mirror. She looked normal, but why didn't she feel normal? Grace never shared the knowledge about her gift of precognition with anyone other than Guy and Mike. She saw the way her community treated her grandmother and she feared being treated the same way. Perhaps the fact they lived in a small town was why her grandmother was treated so differently, but she couldn't be certain. The supernatural may be more tolerated here in New Orleans, but still, she didn't want everyone at the precinct looking at her as if she had a third eye or something. It was bad enough that she, Guy, and Mike were treated differently since they headed up the supernatural section for the precinct. A few detectives believed the mayor was wasting the city's money. Then, there were those who knew better. Between the three of them, they had seen more than anyone else who lived here and what they saw could not simply be explained away. Mike had a difficult time convincing Guy about the possibilities of the supernatural living here in New Orleans, but Grace was easy to convince.

Pulling out of her parking spot, her mind abruptly saw a quick flash of a boy fleeing the woods with shadows chasing after him. The vision only lasted a few seconds. Unlike her other visions, this one lacked any clarity and was over before she could even comprehend what was happening.

She gripped the steering wheel as she calmed her racing heart. This was the first vision that came to her so suddenly and in the middle of the day. Usually, she had to walk the scene in order to have a vision. She had grown accustomed to the victim's emotions barraging her, but this was something more. She not only felt the boy's fear, but the killer's exhilaration.

Once again, a sense of hopelessness came over her. Something evil was coming and she prayed like hell that they could survive it.

As soon as she walked into the precinct a cacophony of sounds barraged her. The sounds were anything but harmonious. Instead, the sounds of the precinct were varied and discordant. The most obvious of sounds was the dozens of human voices; each carrying on an independent conversation. Underneath the conversational clamor, the hum of the copy machine could be heard as it spit out papers and the continuous sound of fingers clacking on keyboards. There was also the sound of doors as well as file drawers opening and closing, shoes slapping against the old linoleum floor and finally the incessant ringing of the phone. Topping it off was the cry of an ill tempered baby on its mother's hip.

Not wanting to be outdone by the sounds was the smell that radiated from a mixture of the older building's pungent odor mixed with the stench of body odors and coffee brewing, which from the smell, it had been cooking for several hours. The only thing keeping anyone from choking on the atmosphere was the ceiling fans running constantly on high speed.

As she made her way down the hall, she saw door after door leading to the various offices for sergeants, detectives, interrogation rooms, conference rooms and storage closets. It took Hutch a while to learn the layout of the precinct, but now that she was used to it, she knew it like the back of her hand.

***

Grace was unsure how she survived the day without anything bad happening, but she did. Perhaps her gut instincts were wrong. As soon as she pulled into her parking space at her apartment complex, Grace was overcome again with a sense of foreboding. It hit her hard, as if someone sucker-punched her in the stomach. Instead of getting out of her car, she gripped the steering wheel and stared out into space.

It was almost as if someone was telling her not to go inside her apartment. She couldn't explain it, she knew something was wrong.

She moved her eyes from side to side, taking in her surroundings. The massive oak trees flanking the complex were no different. She didn't sense anyone lurking behind them. Nothing sinister lurked in the shadows, as far as she could tell. As the sun set on the parking lot, all was quiet.

She turned off her ignition and stepped out of the car. If something was waiting for her, she would soon find out. Opening the front door, she listened for any movement. She could sense the evil all around her, even though she couldn't see it. She could smell its dank odor as it filled the room. Could something be hiding in the shadows waiting to pounce?

As she locked her door, a voice spoke inside of her head. "Hello, Detective."

Grace went still. The voice was deep and resonated, but also seductive and alluring. He slid into her mind like honey; yet, she was bone-chillingly afraid. She tried to block him from her mind, but he was stronger, "Tsk tsk Grace. We need to talk cher. We have a lot to discuss."

Grace tried to ignore her racing heart and the growing sense of dread. She attempted to block him from probing her mind. Finding the strength, she told him, "I don't like you invading my mind and reading my thoughts." In that moment before he could tell her anything else, she was able to block him from her mind. Grace could only hope that he didn't learn anything too important while in there. If he discovered her weaknesses he would use it against her.

***

Joshua was furious. He'd hoped to catch her with her guard down. He would learn more about this woman! They had tap danced around each other for months now and he had yet to learn anything significant about her. He hoped that it was the same with her. However, if she knew his exact location, she would be here, attempting to end his life. No, he knew that their location was safe for now. He had hoped to find out if she knew he was close by, but he could not even answer that question.------

Available in eBook and Paperback

www.ingramcontent.com/pod-product-compliance
Lightning Source LLC
Chambersburg PA
CBHW071755190726

48292CB00003B/985